LASSITER RM.

by

ROBERT KING

Grosvenor House
Publishing Limited

This book is published by
Grosvenor House Publishing Ltd
28-30 High Street, Guildford, Surrey, GU1 3EL.
www.grosvenorhousepublishing.co.uk

A CIP record for this book
is available from the British Library

ISBN 978-1-78148-408-1

About the author :-

Robert (Bob) King is 78 years young and this is his first completed novel with future plans for the character 'Sam Lassiter'.

A multi faceted man who spends a majority of his time either painting or writing with a dash of singing too, along side this he is a volunteer at Poole Hospital Bookshop and has pledged a percentage of any profits from this book to go to the Poole Hospital Fundraising.

Dorset born and lead a well travelled life, with scars and wrinkles to prove it, he then settled back in Dorset in the beautiful town area of Poole and has a daughter, two sons and five grandchildren.

Acknowledgements

I would like to thank four wonderful friends for their support and input into Lassiter RM.

Drew Illman, Heidi King, Sharon Jaques and Sarah Guppy

Whose help and support made it possible for me to complete this, my first novel.

Chapter 1

Samuel Robert Lassiter was a ten year old kid with not too much going for him. He was asthmatic, covered in eczema and had 'sticky-out' teeth that protruded over his bottom lip. Some of his fellow pupils took the mickey and laughed at him behind his back. He struggled with his lessons and spent most of his years at the primary school in 'B' level classes. He did however excel in sports, athletics, soccer and cricket, representing not only his school, but the town at soccer and at county level for cricket.

Sam, much to the chagrin of his father, would never be an academic. Just after his eleventh birthday he failed the examination that would allow him into the grammar school. He joined a secondary modern school and was selected for the 'A' stream, in which he managed to stay for the duration of his education. He continued to impress on the sports field as captain of both the soccer and cricket teams.

Sam left school at age 15 without any academic qualifications and was lucky to have a father at a high management level, getting him a job as an apprentice in the drawing office of Southern Gas. He went to night school and had day release for 3 years, the same length of time he spent at the hospital getting his teeth straightened. He struggled with his exams, just managing to achieve a passing grade and obtain an 'ONC' (Ordinary National Certificate) in mechanical engineering. Sam grew to become a good looking eighteen year old, 5 feet 10 inches tall and weighing in at 12 stone. He had broad shoulders tapering down to a slim waist, Powerful arms and legs together with hands as hard as steel, a result of Karate training.

It was 1940 and World War ll was one year underway. Sam's dad was attached to the local REME battalion in a teaching capacity repairing tanks and vehicles. Sam was 18 years old and decided he wanted to fight, so he went for his medical at the Royal Marine barracks at Eastleigh, lied about his asthma and eczema and was passed 'A1'. In 2 months time he would become a Royal Marine, which would either make him or break him.

Chapter 2

So Sam sporting a short haircut, waved goodbye to his father at Bournemouth West railway station en-route to the Royal Marine training depot at Lympstone in Devon. The little train puffed its way slowly through the Dorset countryside, stopping at every little station on its way to Exeter Central. At one stop he was joined in his carriage by a young lad who looked as hard as nails. He introduced himself as Danny Owen, they shook hands and Danny said 'I'm going to join the Marines', Sam said 'Yep' me too.' They arrived at Exeter Central and took another tiny train to Lympstone where a truck was waiting to take them to their new home for the next 12 weeks.

They all signed in and were directed to 2 Nissan huts with 30 beds in each hut in 2 straight lines. In the beds each side of Sam were Steve Foster from Watford, with a strong London accent and Michael Kerr, a posh talking lad who was in line to be selected for WASB, the officer selection board. Mike was a quiet lad and Sam didn't think he would make it to officers' school. The next day, haircuts for all the new intake and issue of equipment. Sam returned to his bunk and went through all the issued clothing. Vests and pants that would never be used throughout his service, shirts, denims (khaki), boots (SV), boots (Drill), socks and puttee's and a blue beret with a red patch where the Royal Marine badge would be held and finally a battle dress. He carefully folded and hung up all the items issued in his locker above his bed.

The new intake squad 646 lined up outside hut 29 and a Sergeant Crook introduced himself. He was dressed in No' 3's, that's white and red cap, blues and boots that sparkled in the early spring sunshine. We were all dressed in fatigues, shirts, puttee's and drill boots. 'Look at this lot' said Sgt. Crook, pointing to a squad marching by, they look fantastic thought Sam. 'They have been here for 10 weeks and you lot will be better than that.' 646 squad came to a stuttered attention, and ordered to 'Right Turn', 'That's towards the fire depot' said Sgt. Crook, pointing to the right.

Sam took to the life in the Marines like a duck to water and became a Section Leader, the honour awarded to recruits showing leadership potential. To recognize those individuals a red triangle was sewn on to the battle dress sleeve and armband when the dress was fatigues.

As the weeks passed it became apparent that Danny was going to make a fine marine, but Mike Kerr wasn't going to make it. After one speed march Sam returned to his bed space to find Mike lying on his bunk in tears. 'I'm not going to make it Sam' he said, 'Stay close to me and I'll get you through this Mike' said Sam, 'Thanks but no thanks Sam, I'm opting out and leaving in the morning.'

Mike said goodbye to Danny and Sam and left in a large Daimler luxury car with daddy driving. He didn't greet his son, he just threw his case in the boot and charged off, tyres skidding.

Nobby Clarke was the troop Corporal working with Sargent Crook with 626 squad, and was an asshole. The man he targeted most was a guy from Margate called Terry Mitchell. 'Mitch' didn't seem to mind Clarke's remarks and often smiled to himself.

Nobby Clarke was the Marine middleweight boxing champion and had been that for the past 2 years.

A notice was on the NAFFI notice board for men who would like to take part in the elimination boxing bouts. Sam was no boxer, but looking at the list he saw Terry Mitchell's name in the middleweight category, Sam confronted Terry and said 'Are you sure you're not doing this to get back at him for some of his crass remarks?', 'Don't worry Sammy boy, I can put my hands up' said Mitch.

On the parade ground the next day Corporal Clarke suggested that Mitch take a 24 hour pass on fight night to save himself a good hiding, 'I'm just going along to avoid guard duty Corporal' said Mitch. The boxing night finals came along and all of 626 squad attended hoping that Mitch didn't get too much of a hammering. Corporal Clarke was announced and jumped into the ring over the top rope, jigging around and flexing his muscles. Mitch entered the ring in a silk like dressing gown with GB N.B.A. emblazoned on the back. He removed the dressing gown slowly and handed it to Danny who was to be his second.

He revealed blue silk shorts with a white stripe down the side. 'Hold on to my dressing gown Danny, this won't take long.'

The bell sounded and Clarke launched an attack, this was parried easily by Mitch who then began to jab his head off. The corporal threw a long looping left that Mitch easily avoided and returned with a left hook that rocked Clarke. He followed it up with a left hook to the solar plexus and then straightened him up with a left hook to the jaw. The Corporal was out on his feet but a final right cross put Corporal Nobby Clarke out for the count. While a doctor and medic attended to Clarke, Mitch left the arena and along with the rest of 626 squad, went to the NAFFI to celebrate. 'Why do I think you have done that before?' said Sam. 'Before I joined up I was the Southern Area Welterweight Champion' Mitch said smiling, 'He will probably tone down his remarks towards me in the future' said Mitch.

The next day, the 626 were on the parade ground putting the final touches to the Passing Out Parade, when Lieutenant Foster appeared and asked Sgt. Crook to halt the squad. The 626 squad halted as one and were turned left and were ordered to stand easy. 'Recruit Sam Lassiter, one step forward.' he said. Sam came to attention and stepped one pace forward. The Lieutenant fronted him and said 'You recruit Lassiter will report to Colonel Farquason-Keiths office at 0900 hrs tomorrow, are we clear?' 'Crystal sir!' said Sam.

As per Royal Marine etiquette, Sam arrived 5 minutes early for his appointment with the Colonel. He was ushered into his office and told to sit, 'Good morning young Lassiter' the Colonel boomed, 'Good morning sir' said Sam, the Colonel continued, 'Do you know what fast tracking is Lassiter?', 'Athletics or motor racing sir?' Sam offered, 'Close, but no' replied the

Colonel, 'In this time of war, any outstanding recruits are offered the chance of a commission, you meet the criteria' said the colonel. 'A section leader, marksman at rifle and brew-gun, and always in the top 3 around the assault course' said the colonel, 'So what do you think, do you want to be an officer?', 'As long as it's in the Corps sir, I don't want to be shunted into some army unit sir' said Sam. 'I can assure you, you will be coming back to us' 'Then it's a yes sir' said Sam. 'You have 2 weeks of basic training to do, then 6 weeks at the Commando School where you shall receive your green beret, after Commando School, you will have time to prepare yourself for Camberley.' said the Colonel.

As Sam marched to the assault course to join the squad he had a feeling of pride, 'Jesus' he thought, green recruit to an officer in 4 months!. He tagged along with the slower recruits on the assault course, encouraging them to complete the course in the allotted time. The Passing Out Parade of squad 626 was in late July 1940 and was attended by parents and friends. Sam's mum and dad were there and for the first time in his life, Sam thought that his dad was really proud of him. Sam was awarded the trophy for the top recruit of 626.

The lads said their goodbyes to parents and friends, returned to the same hut they had since the beginning of their training 12 weeks ago. The recruitment label was now dropped and they became Royal Marines. So, Marine Sam Lassiter and his friends received a 48 hour pass prior to starting the 6 week course at the Commando School across the river Exe at Bickleigh the following Monday.

Chapter 3

After a nice relaxing 48 hours, Sam joined his squad at the Commando school, to be greeted by a tough looking Sargent in jungle greens and a faded green beret that seemed to be welded to his large head.

'So you think you're fit?' he said, 'You will find muscles you never thought you had.' he said. For the next 6 weeks Sam trained hard, route marches, speed marches, assault courses and the dreaded 'Tarzan' course. Of the thirty men who started to course, only twenty five managed to receive their green berets at the end of the 6 weeks intensive training.

At the end of the commando training, twenty two lads were sent home on a 24 hour pass and told to report to Portsmouth on the following Monday to be posted to a fighting unit in Burma. Sam, along with two other Marines returned to Lympstone, Sam waiting for the officers' course to start at Camberley.

Sam looked at the notice board and saw that volunteers for a parachute course were required, the course was for 4 weeks, that would tie in nicely prior to the start at officers' school. He was accepted for the course and was transported to Abington Airfield by an old Bedford truck for basic parachute training. Abingdon was 7 miles south of Oxford a small town which most people just drove through, two pubs, a hotel and a Railway Junction. The first week was mainly theory; they were instructed on how to fold and prepare a 'chute', and all landing techniques.

The two initial jumps were from a stationary balloon anchored down by a winch and were set at 600 feet and 800 feet. Four men and an instructor sat in a basket with a hole in the middle and raised to 600 feet by an old squeaky winch. When the balloon reached 600 feet it was suitably anchored. It was an eerie feeling, between silent pauses, and the whistling of the wind through the lines holding the balloon to the basket. All five of us hooked on, and then right out of the blue the instructed slipped through the hole in the floor of the basket and was on his way earthbound.

One by one we slipped through the basket, and our first ever jump was over. Sam thought what a wonderful feeling when his 'chute" opened as he drifted towards the ground. All parachute guys yell something at the point of exit from either the balloon or a plane. 'Geronimo' seemed to be the call made by most jumpers. Sam yelled "Bollocks" in between the initial jump and his 'chute' opening. In the afternoon they re-packed the 'chutes' and made their way to the balloon again to make their 800 foot jump. There would be no free fall jumps, all jumps were taken from a stick where you were all hooked up to a line. Four more jumps were made from a de Havilland Hastings aircraft, two from 2000 and two from 4000 feet. Of the ten men on the course six were from 2 Para, 2 from an Army Infantry outfit, an RAF pilot and Sam from the Royal Marines.

The next day an old air force bus drove them to Sam's home town, Poole in Dorset to prepare for the sea jump into the harbour. They were billeted overnight at the Royal Marine Base for swimmer canoeists. Sam met a few of the lads in the NAFFI and came to the conclusion that these were hard men and would go through a wall for you. If Sam ever controlled a Troop of his own he would try to install that kind of mentality in them.

Looking down from 4000 feet the Dorset coastline looked fantastic with the water in the harbour a deep shade of blue, a white foam hitting the beautiful yellow sand of the Sandbanks beaches. The jump went fine and on landing in the sea all jumpers released their chutes and got in line treading water until the Marine with a hoop rope traveling very quickly in a rubber inflatable hoisted them on to the craft.

That evening the whole party was transferred by coach to the Marine Base at Lympstone in readiness for the night jump over Dartmoor. After spending a boring day packing and re-packing their chutes they got the call to get on the bus for the Exeter airstrip.

At 4000 feet they reached the DZ and the call came 'Stand in the Door!'.

"Red light on, Go,Go,Go!'

Everybody was successful, no landing injuries as they collected their chutes and struck out through the barren rough countryside of Dartmoor for the designated pick-up point. All the men received their wings the following morning and apart from Sam all departed to their various regiments. Sam had a week to prepare for the War Office Selection Board (WASB) at the Officers School in Camberley. He got the tailor at Lympstone to sew on his new set of wings and to put the single pip on the shoulder of all his uniforms.

Chapter 4

Sam collected his rail pass from the general office for the journey to Camberley via Poole so he could call in on his parents before going on. The train journey to Camberley was slow and tedious, rain hammering down causing strange patterns on the dirty windows. On arrival he went straight to the Cafeteria on the station, the girl behind the counter whose name tag said Mabel said 'What can I get you luv'?', 'You can get me a nice cup of white coffee please and an egg sandwich'. Said Sam. 'Coming up, I'll bring it over young man', "Cheers".

Sam walked across the little cafe and sat down opposite another young Officer from the Royal Engineers. Sam leaned across the table and said 'Hi, I'm Sam Lassiter Royal Marines.', 'Hi yourself, my name is Templeton, Lance Templeton, Royal Engineers, I'm up for this WASB thing.' Lance Templeton was a huge teddy bear of a man, well over 6 foot and way out of condition. A typical '*Brown Job*' Sam thought. 'I'm here for the same reason, but I don't think I'll get through the course' Sam said, "Academically I'm a loser, I'll murder the physical stuff, speed marches, route marches, long runs, assault courses and any weapon training, but the other more technical stuff I'm buggered.'

'I'll do a deal with you Sam' said Lance, 'I'll get you through the academic stuff if you get me through the physical side of things', 'You've got your self a deal Lance.' said Sam and settled back in his seat taking a sip of coffee. Then the door flashed open and two young thugs entered the cafeteria, "You!" the larger of the two said looking straight at Mabel, 'Shut the fuck up'. The smaller younger kid took station at the cafeteria door while the big fella went up to Lance with a flick knife in his hand and said 'I've been watching you posh boy, now get your money out'. Lance didn't move a muscle, he just sat there and continued to browse the local rag. The man slashed the newspaper in half and half charged towards Sam, this was an error, Sam easily side stepped the rush spinning to his left and launching a vicious kick to the guys head, the guy was out before he hit the floor. 'How brave are you' said Sam looking at the other guy.

'Brave enough to cut you' he said moving towards Sam. Sam picked up a boiling cup of coffee and threw it in the guys face, followed it up by a hard kick straight into the man's groin area. He dropped to the floor in agony holding on to his balls. 'Yes you hold on to them you creep, and count them', said Sam.

'Mabel can you phone the local Bobby to come and sort this lot out and you had better call an Ambulance as well.' said Sam. Sam looked at Lance and said 'You were never going to give him any money were you Lance?', 'No, not when I could leave it up to the Marines.' He laughed.

The local Police arrived along with an Ambulance and after taking statements from Lance, Sam and Mabel, they were allowed to leave. The two young officers signed in at the Guard House and were directed to the Officers Quarters. Sam's room was small, decorated with the normal pale green walls, a bed, a table with a table light and a large locker where Sam hung up his three uniforms, he put all his other clothes neatly folded on the locker shelves. He straightened out his khaki battle dress, gave his boots a bit of a clean and marched across the square to the Officers Club to meet up with his fellow officer recruits. There were only six candidates on the course and only Sam was what was called a "Fast Tracker", the other young officers were very well spoken, beautifully mannered, and obviously ex Public Schoolboys and oozing class. The only odd ball was Sam who was still very conscious of his strong Dorset country boy accent.

When the intake took a look at what was on Sam's arm, the cross rifles and the two light blue wings on his upper arm just beneath his Royal Marine Commando flashes, they greeted him warmly. Captain Jerry Harper would be our mentor for the 4 week course and after introducing himself asked the guys for a quick summary of there life in the services so far. The five guys before him gave splendid presentations, highlighting their Universities and their academic qualifications. Now it was Sam's turn, he stood up and smiled and prepared to address the five officers and his mentor, 'It's sort of after the Lord Mayors Show really' said Sam trying very hard not to be a country "bumpkin". 'I failed my final year of a Higher National certificate in Mechanical Engineering, I talk like I have a bit of straw sticking out of my ear in fact I am what the higher management refer to as a "Fast Tracker". After showing a little promise during my training at the Marine Base in Lympstone and the Commando School in Bickleigh I was fast tracked to Officers School.' 'So, why am I here?'

'Basically I'm as fit as a flea, I have a black belt at Karate, I can jump out of planes, I can run forever and want to kill as many Germans and Japanese as I possibly can, whether as an Officer or a regular Marine.' Sam thought he may have over done it a bit, but what the hell, he meant what he said.

'0800 tomorrow morning gentlemen, Drill with RSM Morgan, You have the rest of the day to yourselves so go walk around and familiarize yourselves with your new surroundings.'

It was a pleasant late summers afternoon as Sam walked the Campus making a mental note of the various buildings, restaurant, gym, cinema, running track and the officers mess. We were square bashing for a week non-stop 0800 to 1600 hours every day, with each officer cadet taking charge of the group with the RSM making copious notes. The team of Lance and Sam was working out OK, Lance was getting fitter by the day being driven hard by Sam, and Lance being patient with Sam with his academic progress. 'We are going to beat this are we not Samuel', said an exhausted Lance, 'We certainly are posh boy', joked Sam.

Sam always looked forward to Thursdays when he was free of all classes and lectures and could devote his time to his studies. He also had time to keep all his gear in tip top condition. He decided to go to the officers mess for a spot of lunch when on passing the NAFFI notice board saw that a dance was advertised for Saturday and that all trainee officers should make a point in attending. Dress: "*Best Blues & White Gear*", the notice said.

Chapter 5

Sam headed for the Canteen and picked up a menu. He reached the serving counter and ordered lamb cutlets, mash and a few veg from a very attractive young lady who unfortunately had a wedding ring on her finger, her name tag said T. Palmer.

Although she smiled at him she still looked sad, 'There you are Lieutenant enjoy your meal' she said. Sam took a seat where he could keep an eye on this pretty lady. A gap appeared in the queue and there was no other person in line to be served, this caught out Sam and he held out his hand and said 'I'm sorry you caught me clocking you'. 'I think you will know me the next time you see me Lieutenant', said a quiet voice. 'I'm sorry' said Sam realising that he had been staring at her, 'I'm new at this game of being an officer and a gentleman', he said. 'Apology accepted' said Mrs. Palmer. 'Come on over and sit down with me', he said pointing to the seat opposite him. Mrs. Palmer looked around to see if any Supervisors or fellow workers were looking, decided not and wandered over and sat at Sam's table. She was even more beautiful close up with fair wavy hair protruding from under non-flattering head gear and sparkling blue eyes.

'It's nice to rest my poor old feet' she said. 'If you weren't a married lady Mrs. P I'd ask you to the dance on Saturday', 'With all these pretty Army, Air Force and Nurses here on base you have plenty of girls to chose from', she said, 'By the way Sam, my name is Trisha', she said,' Just over a year ago my husband who was a Sergeant Weapons Instructor at Catterick, was killed by an accidental discharge from a Sten' Gun from one of his recruits' she said. 'I have not been out of the house in the evening for over a year' she said. 'Shit, I should have kept my big mouth shut, I'm so sorry' said Sam. She rose from her seat and walked slowly away from the table, she turned and said 'Do you still want to take me to the dance Lieutenant?', 'Very much' said Sam.

She went back to the serving counter and scribbled a note, returned to Sam's table and dropped the note on the table, 'See you tomorrow night Sam' as she disappeared into the kitchen. Sam returned to his room and crammed, he studied all the rest of the day until early evening, what he didn't know now, he would never know. He stood up and said to himself that he was ready for his final exam the following morning.

He met Lance at the Athletics Field and they completed a three mile run. Once Sam got over the eerie silence that greets any exam sitter, he was good and ready to go. He struck lucky with the exam paper, the questions slotting in nicely with what Lance told him to focus on. Lance looked over to Sam and winked, when the four hour exam paper finished all the officer cadets adjourned to the mess, the majority of the lads were happy with the exam paper. Sam went over to Lance and said 'Thanks buddy I nailed it'.

At 7pm on the Saturday evening Sam took a taxi to Union Street, stopped outside 34a and told the driver to wait. Sam knocked the door and almost immediately Trisha was there, looking sensational. 'Your escort to the ball Madam' said Sam. 'Thank you Lieutenant', she replied in a pseudo posh accent. Sam checked them both in at the Guard House and they boarded the bus that would take them to the building where the dance was being held. Even in the dimly lit bus interior Sam could see the natural beauty of the young lady sitting next to him. Trisha checked in her coat and scarf and Sam his white hat with the red band. As Trisha moved away from the clothing drop she stopped and looked at Sam. 'What' she said, Trisha was standing directly in front of him in a little black dress which ended two inches above her knees, a strap over each shoulder, a black choker and black stiletto shoes. 'Stunning', said Sam.

They moved into the Ballroom together, Trisha resting her hand on Sam's arm. Sam saw the tall figure of Lance and the other guys who had snared a table nicely tucked away in a corner. The four officers were being entertained by a tall attractive young lady, and whatever she was saying went down like a storm as they all fell about laughing. As Sam and Trisha approached the table all the small talk stopped, and the five guys stood open mouthed at the shear beauty of the lady before them.

They all sat down at the corner table and the young lady was the first to speak. 'Hi I'm Katherine Templeton, Lance's sister, it's nice to meet you Sam, I've heard so much about you from my brother, he's been talking about you for weeks' 'Lance, close your mouth' she continued. Lance couldn't take his eyes off Trisha.

Trisha could see straight away that Lance was embarrassed and very shy and stretching out her arms before her approached Lance and said, 'Come on Lance, let's dance', and pulled him on to the dance floor. That gesture broke the ice and the party got underway, the four remaining lads in the group made for the Nurses' table, which left Sam alone with Katherine Templeton. 'Lance talks a lot about you Sam and how you two got together after a little argument at the railway station', said Katherine. 'Your brother showed a lot of "bottle" that night Katherine'. Said Sam. 'Before he left for officer school he told me that he thought he would have trouble with the physical stuff as he was so unfit', she said. 'It was a two way thing Katherine, I would assist in getting him fit and he would guide me through the academic stuff, It worked we are now officially true Officers', 'He has also become my best friend' said Sam. Your date tonight is a very beautiful girl Sam, she looks stunning', 'I didn't realise how lovely she was until tonight' said Sam.

'Come on Lieutenant Lassiter, let's dance' said Katherine. Trisha and Lance returned to the table and Lance, always the gentleman, showed her to her seat along side Sam. Sam leaned closer to her and whispered in her ear 'That was a very nice, kind thing you did to get Lance out of a bit of a hole'. 'Not a problem, now I can devote my entire evening to the guy that brought me here', said Trisha.

The evening was progressing nicely with Sam and Trisha inseparable, Lance was pre-occupied with a young Nurse and his sister taking the whole situation in her stride, conversing with the established older Officers and their wives. The four other officers in our group were systematically working there way through a bunch of willing Nurses. A General approached Sam and Trisha at there table introduced himself and sat down,

'What did you think of the course Lieutenant?' He said. 'At first I wasn't sure Sir, I didn't seem to fit in with the rest of the lads, but they and the Instructors made sure I was part of the team. The content of the course I thought focused a tad to much on the art of being an officer and a gentleman and not enough on the various methods of killing the enemy. Unarmed combat skills should be taught to all officers whether Marines or not sir. But basically the course was fantastic and the standard of teaching, outstanding', said Sam. 'That's good to hear young Lassiter, one more thing…, is it a Royal Marine thing that you get the prettiest girl in the room', said the General. 'I think she took pity on me Sir, being the only country "bumpkin" on the course.

The General laughed and moved on to complete his circulation duties. Sam and Lance went to the bar to fetch some more drinks for the girls, which left Katherine and Trisha alone at the table. 'I wish I could be more like you Katherine, holding interesting intelligent conversations, and speaking such perfect English', said Trisha. 'Many thousands of daddy's pounds for a classic education at a girls college' said Katherine.

'I tell you what though Trisha I'd give all the education and fancy talk up if I could look like you', said Katherine. 'I work as a server in the officers mess hardly a glamorous occupation, and not likely to be called to appear at Deb of the year', she said.'

'Although you are a lovely looking girl, I suppose it doesn't really matter what you look like really or what you do for a living, or how you talk, it's just about being a nice person Trisha and you are a very nice person with a heart as big as a house', she said. They both stood up and gave each other a hug and hooked little fingers saying that they would be friends and keep in touch.

'What do you think of Sam? said Katherine, 'He is a nice, kind caring sort of a guy and he makes me laugh, which is something I haven't done for a long time Katherine and between you and me he's kind of cute', she said. 'More than cute Trisha, he's bloody gorgeous' said a laughing Katherine. 'We have two weeks together before he goes off to fight those dreadful Japanese and I intend to give him all the love and attention during that time'.

He was telling me that the life expectancy of a junior officer in the Burma campaign isn't so good, but he would change these odds and come back home when it was all over. Lance and Sam arrived back at the table with the drinks just in time for the last waltz. Sam and Trisha danced together, Lance with his pretty little Nurse and Katherine with an old Officer who was a friend of her Father. The final bars of the last waltz faded away and the band stood and played the National Anthem.

Chapter 6

As they left everybody swapped addresses and phone numbers, said there goodbyes and made there way home. Sam and Trisha took a taxi back to Union Street paid the man and entered Trisha's little house. Neither of them said a word as they sat down close to each other on her sofa. Sam very gently eased her forward and kissed her, Trisha responded passionately.

Trisha broke off the kiss and said 'I'm going to change Sam, you relax I won't be long', Sam took off his clothes and sat on the sofa looking like a kid in detention, wearing only his boxers. Trisha returned to the lounge wearing a white robe and sat down close to Sam, kissed him gently on the lips and Sam responded with much more passion. 'Don't expect too much Sam, it's been a long time', she said. Sam leaned forward again and slipped the dressing gown off her left shoulder to reveal two perfectly formed breasts, which he caressed and kissed until her nipples stood proudly out.

'I must warn you Trisha I'm the world's worst lover', said Sam escorting her to the bedroom. They made love and it was a disaster, Sam's premature ejaculation problems still apparent as he shot semen all over Trisha's belly and on the pristine sheets. 'I'm so sorry, failed again' said Sam. 'Nothing to worry about' said Trisha cleaning up the mess on her tummy and on the bed clothes. 'Lets rest a little and try again later and this time you can wait for me', she said. They made love twice more that night and it was wonderful with Sam doing all the right things and coordinating climax times with Trisha.

'I could get used to this' said Sam, 'Me too', she said.

The following morning Sam showered gave the sleeping Trisha a peck on the cheek and left her place to return to his room on the campus. They saw each other every day of the two weeks before the scheduled ending of the course. She attended the pass out parade to see Sam classified as a bone-fide Lieutenant.

Sam looked the business in his number one dress as he took the salute with his dress sword. The pass out over, all six guys were greeted by their families. Sam's mum and dad couldn't make it but Trisha was there for him. Sam and Trisha were introduced to all the now fully fledged officer's parents and friends. Sir Keith Templeton, Lance's dad was there with his beautiful young wife Lady Janet and of course the party girl Katherine.

Trisha looked a little sad as she caught up with Sam and drew him aside. She whispered 'I know you are off tomorrow bound for Burma to link up with 44 Commando and that I may not see you again, but can I say one thing, you have brought a little happiness into my life again and for that I will never forget you Sam. 'Luv yah to bits' she said grabbing his arm as they set off circulating and doing the things that officers are supposed to do.

On the morning he was due to leave he wrote a note to Trisha and dropped it into the post box by the guard house. He turned and prepared to get into the staff car, when Trisha appeared, she didn't say a thing just walked up to him and gave him a huge hug, she then turned and walked away in tears.

Sam sat on the back seat and as they made their way slowly to the main gate, he looked out of the rear window and saw Trisha standing all alone waving a tiny Union Jack.

Chapter 7

The staff car turned to the left and set out for Northolt Airport on the A4 in North West London. Sam was provided space on a Dakota DC7 transport plane going to India, via Zurich, Beirut and finally Calcutta.

Sam's orders were to report to the Royal Marine 44 Commando, 3rd Brigade Burma Campaign. This was the unit that specialised in Amphibious Landings. Sam landed in Calcutta and was met by a cheerful little fella who was with the Special Forces and was known locally as "Chin Dits". These men were top rated for fighting in jungle warfare and were attached to the British Indian Forces, he was taken to the base where he received his orders and flight time for his 1100-mile trip to Burma. The Commanding Officer then gave Sam a brief history of the conflict in Burma, he said that the Japanese initial intention was to capture Rangoon the capital and principal seaport, this would close the overland supply line to China, the Japanese have successfully attacked Kawkareik Pass and the Port of Moulmein, 'We had to pull back our troops to India regroup, we have only recently returned to Burma'.

After a long, tedious, uneventful flight the old aircraft bumped and bounced on the temporary runway and came to a halt 50 metres from a terminal that looked more like an over sized caravan with aerials poking out of the roof. He travelled by bus from the Airport to the Nhila Base Terminal close to the Tek Naf Peninsular, where he was met by a young 2nd Lieutenant called Steadman who escorted Sam to his new home on the base.

Sam was introduced to Captain Brian Foster the 'A' Troop Commander. 'Lieutenant Steadman will look after sections 1 and 2, and you Mr. Lassiter will take charge of sections 3 an 4. Good luck and good hunting', the Captain concluded and closed the meeting. Sam walked down to the area where 'A' Troop was billeted and asked one of the Marines to direct him to Colour Sergeant Len Jackson. 'He's in Hut 57 sir taking a weapons class', the young Marine said. Sam entered Hut 57 and immediately Colours shouted "Attention". 'Carry on Colours', said Sam.

The weapons training session ended and Colours said 'Would you like to say a few words Sir'. Sam moved to the front of the class and said 'As you can see I'm still a bit green around the ears and my knees aren't brown yet, so I have a lot to learn about fighting out here and making sure that we all get through this. As you can see, (pointing to his cross rifles and parachute wings) I can shoot straight and I'm not scared of heights. I'm aware however that I have a lot to learn', 'Colours, a private word please' said Sam.

'Off the parade ground and out of earshot Colours my name is Sam'. 'Yes Sir'. Said Colours. Sam continued 'I want to learn all about tactics, stealth, hygiene, diet and the more I learn about jungle warfare the better. With your help Colours I want 'A' Troop back on top again after all the shit they have had during the last few months'.

'OK we start tomorrow 0700 lets take the lads on a 3 mile run and enjoy the Burma countryside", said the Colour Sergeant.

The following morning sections 3 and 4 assembled outside there hut and lined up in columns of three. Sam attached himself to the rear of the group and fell in line. 'Sections Right Turn, double March' said Colours, and off they went. After the run Colours addressed the men, 'Jungle Greens tomorrow and clean your weapons, I'll be inspecting them at first light', he said. The Colour Sergeant dismissed the men and walked across to talk to Sam, 'I think that went well Sir', he said. 'It's a start' said Sam 'I'm taking the lads into he Jungle tomorrow sir why don't you come along?' '0700, I'll be there Colours'.

Sam strolled leisurely back towards his quarters when he saw a young lad attending to an old lady who seemed to have collapsed in a ditch. 'Is she OK young man?' said Sam, 'She's fine, she's bruised her legs, that's all' said the young man.

'What's your name young man', said Sam to the tiny skinny kid.

'Jonny Li, one day Doctor Li' he said.

Sam flagged down a passing jeep and told the driver to take the old lady and the young man to the sick bay. 0700 Sections 3 and 4 moved out all men looking good in jungle greens and black webbing. They left the well worn track about a mile from the base and set foot into the jungle. Jesus Lieutenant you're like a "Fuckin" carthorse' Said Colours, 'Tread lightly and use the outside of your feet'.

It was 100 degrees and probably 90% humidity, Sam had never felt so uncomfortable in his life. After 6 hours of cutting their way through dense jungle they returned to base. Sam walked slowly to his room got in his cot under the mosquito net and crashed out.

Sam was determined not to make a fool of himself again in front of the lads, so he took steps to make improvements. He befriended two "Chin Dits" who are known as excellent jungle fighters and asked questions and got answers. An operation for 'A' Troop was set up for the day after tomorrow, all 4 sections would be involved. Sam checked out his gear and weapon for the mission and rested for the rest of the day.

He passed a nurse as he was going to the canteen who stopped and said, 'Lieutenant you remember that young lad that you brought to the sick bay', 'Yes I remember him very well' said Sam, 'Well, he seemed so interested in all that was going on in the sick-bay I gave him one of my books on Anatomy and told him to have a read'. She said. 'The kid has talent, I asked him questions on various aspects of anatomy and he answered every one perfectly. He returned the book to me and I loaned him another on Chemistry, he said he would be back to answer any questions next week'.

Sam's first action came 3 weeks later when, while on Patrol, contact was made with noisy Japanese soldiers slashing their way through the jungle and had wandered off their targeted area. Colour Sergeant Jackson heard them first and raised his arm which meant everybody freeze. As the japs came into our space they were met by a barrage of machine gun fire which cut them to pieces. Fifteen bodies were left lying twitching on the jungle floor. 3 section finished off the three Jap's that were still breathing. 'No prisoners then Colours', said Sam. 'Have you seen what these bastards do to our POW's sir', said Colour Sergeant Jackson, 'I can guess Colours' said Sam. 'They torture, burn, cut off limbs and execute our boys with a "Fuckin" Samurai sword', said Colours. On returning to base Sam felt no remorse for the non-taking of prisoners. He made contact with the Senior Nurse again and enquired on young John Li's progress. 'The kid's a natural, not only in his studies he is always around to help out when things get busy with incoming wounded', she said, 'How much would it cost to get the kid to the states to study', said Sam, 'I think I could get him into my old College Hospital in Santa Barbara 'for a least the first year for I guess $5000.' 'Set it up Nurse and for his baby Sister too, I'll pay', said Sam.

Within a month John and his baby sister were on their way to the States and to a future beyond their wildest dreams. 'Don't let me down John and take care of "Spud" the nickname he had used for John's grubby faced little sister.

Chapter 8

As the Burma Campaign went into it's third year the Allies were maintaining steady progress driving the Japanese into deeper defensive positions making it harder to flush them out. Sam had been promoted to Captain and had taken over as 'A' Troop Commander. His troop had become the elite of 44 Commando with many medals issued for gallantry. It was late 1943 when Sam and Colour Sergeant Jackson received orders to report to the Commanding Officers office. The C.O. sat at the head of the long table with Sam on one side and Colours on the other, they were later joined by a Captain Clarke from the Intelligence Section.

'Thirty miles from here the Japanese have secured a focal point and are well established, they are causing havoc to our Navy boys passing through the straights.' said the C.O. Giving Captain Clarke the nod to continue. He showed some aerial pictures of the Japanese Base and pointed out 3 black images, 'These I think are Howitzers converted by the Jap's to be very effective against our Navy Fleet, The two additional little black items here, look under a magnifying glass to be captured American Lewis guns used to back up the Howitzers, We estimate 200 to 230 Japanese on the base and around 50 British POW's'.

The C.O interrupted the Captain and said 'Get me a plan to get these bastards out by tomorrow say 10.30 hours'.

'I'll work with Colour Sergeant Jackson and the "Chin Dits" and have something ready in the morning. He picked up the photos and left the building.

He returned to the C.O.'s office early the next morning and presented the plan no the Colonel to take down the Japanese Base at Mye Bon. 'How do you rate your chances of pulling this off Lieutenant? said the C.O. 'It's all about timing sir, if we can take out the mobile patrol and the guards at the Howitzer's and co-ordinate these with the destruction of the Japanese living quarters, we've got to be looking at an 80% success for the mission', said Sam. "As far as casualties are concerned 'A' Troop has a fine record and I intend to keep it that way, everybody in, do the job and everybody out', said Sam. They all stood up and were just about to leave when the Colonel turned to Sam and said, Congratulations Sam orders came through today; as from 0800 today you have been promoted to Major'. 'Thank you sir', said Sam.

Sam assembled the men he had chosen for the mission and set out clearly their individual tasks. He produced a note for Colours, told him to check it and then go ahead and acquire the equipment needed for the raid. Sniper Scopes, Binoculars, Dynamite, Blasting Caps, Detonator Cord, Plungers, Grenades (Fragmentation), extra ammo 9mm and 303, First Aid Kits and finally four Rubber Inflatable boats.

At 2100 hours the following evening the team of 24 men left he base in a Landing Craft that would take them the first 15 miles towards their target. After nearly 2 hours the Landing Craft Pilot killed the engine and the craft slowly came to a halt, the rubber boats were lowered over the side of the craft and six men per inflatable crowded into the four boas, as the Marines quietly paddled away the landing craft turned and was on her way back to base.

The next eight miles took a lifetime, the six men in each boat sharing the paddling. It was close to midnight when they reached the selected landing area pushing the inflatables into secure areas, tying them down and covering them with camouflage nets and bamboo canes.

The team spread out and moved forward with Sam taking the lead and the Colour Sergeant taking point. Moving through the jungle was a lot easier than Sam had envisioned, it was obvious that the Japanese had been through this area before slashing their way through the undergrowth. The team arrived at the target location, each man to his allotted position. Although it was 3am the humidity was up to 90% and making things uncomfortable. Sam did a visual and was satisfied that all the men were nicely ensconced in position, he used his binoculars to pinpoint the three Howitzer's that looked menacing and ghost like and the two Lewis guns perched on rocks each side of the big guns.

One guard patrolled between the three Howitzer's, while two man mobile teams lapped the camp perimeter. The time read 3.35 am when Sam whispered to Len Jackson 'We wait until sun up at 4am then we make our move'. The guard change at 4am took place as they strolled around the perimeter fence. The first patrol passed within feet of Marines Holloway and Jones and as they passed the two Marines struck, grabbing the guards from behind and sliding there 8 inch blades across their throats. The second mobile patrol was dealt with in he same manner by the "Chin Dits".

Sam and Colours took care of the sleepy looking guards of the Howitzer's, easing them back on to an 8 inch blade. They both took large spanners to the Howitzers and removed the breech loading gear and threw them into the Gulf and finally working their way to the Lewis Guns. The sun was just peering over the horizon when Sam received signals from the men that all high explosives were in place on the four temporary accommodation blocks.

The sun was more or less up now, shining across the base making it look like it was on fire. Four pairs of eyes were watching Sam through binoculars waiting for the signal to light up the Japanese base. Sam raised his arm high and then dropped it quickly to his side. Four large explosions erupted and four buildings were destroyed by the blast and by fire. All four of the temporary buildings were on fire and any Japanese soldiers still alive were making there way out of the buildings, some completely naked and some with that little white table cloth covering there genitals and rear end. They were greeted by mass small arms fire from two Bren' Gunners and six Sten' gunners, all the Japanese were struck down.

Sam and Len Jackson opened up with the Lewis guns completely destroying the officer's hut and the fuel and ammunition storage areas. Then an eerie quiet with a few groans from the dead or dying Japanese, some still twitching in the last throws of death.

'What the hell is that' said Colour Sergeant Jackson, looking at a very artistic sand sculpture in front of some kind of cave. Just as Sam was going to explore this oddity, about 30 Japanese Soldiers came out of the cave in various states of dress, falling in line behind an officer holding high a white flag that was tied to a rifle. 'Round them up and sit them down', said Sam. Sam drew his regulation 9mm Browning, went down the incline and entered the cave, what he saw he would remember for the rest of his life. There were severed arms and legs piled in one corner, on the left hand side of the building there were 6 stakes with a head rammed down on each, a Samurai sword lay close by, Sam could see the pain etched on all the grotesque faces on the British POW's. He left the cave and was violently sick. 'I want all the guys to go in there in pairs and look what these people have done', 'Collect all of the dead guys dog tags' said Sam. He turned to face his men who had been visibly affected by the death cave, 'Fuck the Geneva Convention, execute the prisoners' said Sam picking up a Bren' gun and together with his team sprayed the prisoners with gunfire until nobody moved. 'Get on the radio Taff, mission accomplished', said Sam.' 'A' Troop to base, over'. Said Taff, 'Base here go ahead 'A' Troop Mission accomplished you can move in when you like the Japanese base now belongs to us, come up the Gulf the Howitzers are no longer a threat.' 'Roger to that 'A' troop, out.

Sam's first aider's got busy cleaning up the POW's as best they could applying clean dressings to their open wounds. In the early afternoon troops and temporary buildings arrived as the new forward base was established. Sam recalled the two Rocket Launcher and two Bren' Gun teams that he had positioned under cover alongside the one and only road in and out of the Japanese Base.

'A message from Major Lassiter, over.' said Taff the radio operator. 'Howitzer's and Lewis guns destroyed, many Japanese dead, will count bodies, will advise over.'

'Roger that A Troop, a message from the Colonel to Major Lassiter, over.' 'Colonel Stanfield here, well done Sam. God job. Over.'

'Roger that Colonel, message passed on to the Major. Over and out.', said Taff.

A radio message later said that troops had left the base and were due to arrive in a few hours. In the meantime A troop dug in. After stacking the bodies of the Japanese soldiers 100 yards away at the edge of the jungle. The dead were attracting flies and mosquito's which was the reason for moving the bodies. The following morning B,C and D fighting troops arrived as an advanced party preparing for the main body of troops to arrive.

The following morning, B, C and D fighting troops arrived and set up camp. Sam regrouped his troop and they boarded a landing craft, the C.O was there to greet them. 'Splendid job Major and well done A troop.' he beamed. 'Sorry about the smell sir' said Sam saluting. 'Come and see me when you have cleaned up.' said Colonel Lewis.

Chapter 9

Sam told the Colour Sergeant to dismiss the men and they both slowly made their way to their quarters caked in blood, camouflage cream, sweat and mud. 'I think we could pull a couple of nurses dressed like this sir what do you think?' said Colours. 'I think my perfume should do it, *eau de la shit-house*' said Sam laughing 'see you later, Len',

'Roger that, Major.' said Colours.

In the three days that Sam and his troop were away, the Royal Engineers based at the camp had been busy erecting small portable prefabricated units for officers and senior NCO's. Sam was directed to is new cosy little home. He took off all his clothes and put them in a bag to be thrown away. He stood in the officer's shower for ages in the tepid water and scrubbed himself all, over making his skin red. He returned to his little room and put on a clean t-shirt, underwear and shorts. He laid on this bed under the mosquito net and was sound asleep in seconds.

He awoke at 2100 hours feeling a lot better, He sat on his only chair at the small table and started to write his report on the completed mission. A marine messenger popped his head in Sam's cabin 'A message for Major Lassiter' he said.

'That's me' Sam replied, as the messenger handed the note over 'thanks.'

It was a note from the Colonel, the debrief, his office at 0800 hours tomorrow.

Sam recalled and wrote down everything that had happened. Sam completed his report by midnight and then climbed into his cot and slept soundly until the morning.

Chapter 10

At 0755 hours Sam was seated in Colonel Lewis' RM office as the other officers were ushered into seats around a large old table with a high polish.

'Let's go around the table and introduce ourselves.' said the Colonel. The attendees all introduced themselves one by one. Sam was particularly interested in one of the Officers who introduced himself as Commander Stanton and the guy sitting next to him in civvies who called out his name as Richard Dunwoody, Admiralty. The Colonel explained that the two officers were there purely in an observation capacity.

'Major Lassiter, the floor is yours!' boomed the Colonel.

'First before we get down to the nitty gritty of the operation, I would like to congratulate Captain Lewis and the 'I' section for providing such superb, accurate information on the target area, troop numbers, weaponry and the layout of the Japanese camp.'

Sam then proceeded to read through the de-brief from embarking on the landing craft, swapping to inflatables, taking out the Howitzers and Lewis guns and killing the Japanese soldiers.

'In summary', he said, 'three Howitzer guns destroyed, their breach mechanisms somewhere at the bottom of the Gulf. Two Lewis guns with ammo captured, 257 Japanese soldiers killed, no prisoners taken. No injuries or deaths to 'A' troop personnel.'

'Any questions?' the Colonel said addressing all present. The overweight Major of an infantry regiment said in a sarcastic manner 'Do you expect us to believe that twenty four men took on a Japanese base and killed over two hundred and fifty men Major Lassiter? I suggest you go back to your cabin and re-write your brief!' he continued 'my men have been fighting the Jap's for six months and they have not killed as many as you and your men have claimed to in three days, it's Bullshit and you know it is!' he sat down his face red with anger and frustration.

Sam stood up and said quietly 'Maybe your tactics need looking at Major, I will be looking at new ways to beat these bastards with the Colonel later today.'

'One more thing' he said 'In case the Major has put any doubt in your minds about the mission', he reached under the table and pulled out two hundred and fifty seven Japanese blood stained dog tags from his holdall and threw them across the table. They skidded on the highly polished surface and landed in the lap of the overweight Major, 'Ship them to Fuckin Tokyo!' said Sam.

'Captain Lassiter you stay behind, we need to talk.' said the Colonel and the army officers trooped out of the office leaving behind the Colonel and two of the high ranking Navy Officers and Sam.

The quiet man in the suit spoke to Sam and said 'We are recommending you Major Lassiter and Colour

Sergeant Jackson to both be awarded the Victoria Cross for your honour and bravery in this mission. The decision will be made when we return to our base in India, but be assured, the awards will be made.'

'I don't know what to say Sir.' said Sam, 'Say nothing Sam, well done, oh 'and watch your temper Captain' he said jokingly.

Sam couldn't believe what had just happened and hurried away to locate his Colour Sergeant.

'A' Troops two first aider's got busy assisting the Nurses in carefully moving the wounded into the O R. Sam caught up with Colour Sergeant Len Jackson outside the NAFFI and suggested they go in for a pint.

'You shouldn't be seen drinking with a lowly NCO, Major' said Colours, 'I've got some reasonably important news Colours.' said Sam. 'Go for it.' said Colours, 'The lads have been awarded the military medal for their efforts on the mission' said Sam 'They deserve it sir' said Colours.

'The other little tit bit of information, is that both you and I have been awarded the Victoria Cross!' Sam said smiling 'Jesus Christ.' said the Colour Sergeant.

Chapter 11

The following week on the parade ground all the fighting troops from the Royal Marines and Army Infantry were lined up in threes. 'A' troop were up front wearing green beret's, battle dress and black gear, boots, belt, gaiters and rifle slings. A Major General with not too much room left on his chest for any more medals, presented 'A' troop with their military medals and with the naval general service medals. Major Samuel Lassiter and Colour Sergeant Len Jackson were isolated from the squad and presented with the Victoria Cross. It was the proudest moment of Sam's life. All Colour Sergeant Jackson could say was 'I bet my kids will love this.'

The two men, Sam and Len were headline news and war correspondence wouldn't leave them alone. So Sam, along with Len Jackson, came to an arrangement with the Marine Press Officers. They would hold a one off interview with the press as long that it was understood that on its completion, neither Sam nor Len would be harassed any more.

The gym on base was set up for the press conference on the following day at 1000 hours. When Sam and Len entered the building the following morning they were greeted by twenty reporters from the major paper publishers in the UK. There were camera men and a guy setting up a movie camera.

'OK lets get this show going, said the Marine press officer.

'Fred Colling, Daily Mirror. The Japanese radio and propaganda machine has quoted that the leader of 'A' troop and his right hand man, that's you two gentlemen, are ex London Hoodlums and were involved in major crimes on Civvie Street and your men were all low life criminals and really vicious individuals, is that correct?.'

'Do you want to get that Major?' asked Colour Sergeant Jackson.

'The most part of this, which is incidentally the first time I have heard it, is ridiculous, in fact the normal rubbish coming over Japanese radio. The vicious thing is more or less right, don't you think Colours?' he said as Len gave him an agreeing nod. 'Except' Sam added ''A' troop and its command is ten times worse than vicious.'

'Colin Clark, The Herald. Where are your home towns and do they know of your heroics?' 'I'm from Poole in Dorset, born next to the Marine barracks' said Sam. 'I'm a Yorkshire lad, born and bred in Halifax, south Yorkshire.' Colours added. 'It would be nice if you big hitters would ensure that our local newspapers get to know about the raid.' said Sam. 'I'll make sure they do, Major' the Herald reporter replied. 'Karen Wilson, The Daily Express, Have you guys got wives and kids or girlfriends back in the UK?' Sam looked at Len and gestured him to go ahead. 'I've got a lovely wife, a Yorkshire lass and two boys who I haven't seen for two years' he said. 'And you Major?' Karen asked. 'I was an ugly youth and I'm not much better now! I have both my parents alive and kicking back home who I haven't seen for three years. I met a beautiful girl at Officers school in Camberley and we spent a wonderful month together before I had to report to the 44th in Burma.'

'Ted Thatcher, The Times. What did you feel like after causing all that carnage? Any remorse?', 'Tell them what we saw Captain' interrupted the Colour Sergeant ''After I saw arms and legs scattered all over the place, P.O.W's tortured and then six heads of British soldiers mounted on pedestals, no Mr Thatcher not one ounce of remorse.' Len added more to this. 'I took every Marine in the raiding party to see what the Jap's had done to our fellow Marines' he said, 'some had a tears in their eyes and some vomited, but a lesson was learnt that day.' he finished.

After around an hour the questions stopped, the cameras finished clicking and the movie makers packed up. The marine press officer reminded the reporters that no further harassment of the Major and Colour Sergeant would occur. Both the Victoria Cross holders returned to their huts and prepared a presentation for the Colonels of various regiments at the base. Sam and Len got together to compare notes and agreed on the format of the presentation.

Chapter 12

Everybody sat down at the table and Sam began his presentation. 'It was becoming obvious that small parties of troops, say twenty four men, were the way to go.' 'They could be in and out prior to the main troops arriving, I would suggest each brigade select specialist men, the snipers, Bren' gunners and light machine gunners and good men at unarmed combat.' "A' troop would be a leader in this and assist in the training of these special sections. Small groups can move more quickly and quietly through the jungle and when they reach the target area, hit hard and then retreat.'

It was unanimously decided that a program would be put together to train the selected personnel. Major Lassiter and Colour Sergeant Len Jackson would head up the training program. It was a very peaceful situation for Sam and Len to be instructors and away from the heat of battle, but they were both getting itchy feet to return to the real action.

Chapter 13

The war in Burma was progressing slowly, but the allied forces were still moving north and the Japanese were being pushed further north wards. The Americans were still getting large numbers of deaths in the Philippines.

'Mail call Major Lassiter' said the postie on his rounds, Sam had four letters. The first one was from the Home Office. It read; "*We are very sorry to inform you that your Father has been killed at his place of work. A German bomb hit the canteen at the gas company killing twenty five civilians and unfortunately your Father was one of them. We send our condolences*" Although he wasn't close to his Dad, it was still such a terrible blow. He put down the letter and closed his eyes in quiet meditation. He opened the second letter that was dated three months ago and had finally caught up with him. It was from Trisha.

"*Darling Sam,*

It's been three years since our dinner dance date at the Officers School in Camberley. I can remember every moment as though it was yesterday. I have met a young man called Trevor, who has a nice safe job at the

Camberley Officers School and we are going to get married. You remember you told me to meet a nice guy with a safe job and settle down, well I have and I am very happy.

So Take care of yourself Sam, I will never forget you and the wonderful four weeks we had together.
*   My love as always, Trisha"*

An added note on the letter read: "*Your Mother, who is suffering from premature Alzheimer's has been moved to a home and is being attended by trained nurses. Her sister is taking care of all things financial*".

He was pleased that Trisha had found a nice guy, he would write back to her soon.

The third letter was postmarked London and he had no idea who would write to him from town. He looked at the end of the letter first. It was from Katherine, Lance's sister. "*Hi Sam, just to let you know what's happening on this side of the world*". The letter was written only three weeks ago, it was brilliant that it had arrived so quickly in Burma.

"*Lance is in France and doing very well. He has been promoted to Captain and is serving somewhere in France. You will know by now that Trisha got married, I was her maid of honour. It was a lovely wedding and she looked gorgeous and very happy did our Mrs. Trisha Jevons. You know she did what you told her to do Sam, she married a nice guy with a safe job, his name is Trevor.*

I'm still working at the Admiralty on secret stuff that I'm not allowed to talk about and I'm enjoying it. I'll be glad when it's finally all over. My office has predicted late Summer 1945, for the Germans and the Japanese will surrender. If you have the time please answer this letter and when it's all over maybe we can share a coffee back in the UK.

Love Katherine."

He opened the final letter with his commando knife and saw that it was from Santa Barbara, California, USA. It was from Jonny Li, the young lad who used to help with the cleaning of the gear and washing, for which he made sure he was paid. He wanted to be a doctor but didn't have the necessary qualifications in his native Burma. He helped the nurses on the base and they all called him Doctor Li. The money that Sam had paid for John and "Spud" to go to the US to study was well worth it as his studies were going well at Santa Barbara General. He wrote:

"My studies are over and I am now a qualified Doctor. I live in Santa Barbara with my own surgery specializing in plastic surgery, making women think they look more beautiful than they did before any operations. Please come and visit me in the US, it would be great to see you."

The training program was going well, but Sam and Len were getting edgy requiring a bit of action of their own. They booked an appointment with the Colonel's secretary for 1400 hours that day. Sam made a note in his little black book of all the addresses. He would reply to all four of the letters tomorrow. "I have posted a cheque to the US bank in Calcutta, so if you could get your transport guys who regularly fly to India to cash the money and give it back to you. Goodbye. Li"

Chapter 14

They sat down opposite the Colonel and Sam said 'We are being treated like a protected species, when are we going to be returning to the real thing?' Len the Colour Sergeant nodded in the direction of the Colonel. 'Some good news gentlemen the Japanese have sustained massive losses in Pyanbwe after our lads had outflanked them, many of the fleeing Jap's have been drowned crossing the river Sittang on bamboo floats. It was a triumph for the British Indian Army. The Burma Campaign gentlemen is nearing completion.'

'You are not returning to action, either of you.' he said. 'The war in Burma is getting closer to closure, the Allies are making rapid progress in Europe, the Russians are beating the hell out of the Germans on the Eastern front and finally the Americans are slowly working their way northwards through the Philippine Islands. I believe along with a few egg heads at HQ that the war will be over before this winter.'

'I have had new orders in today for you both' the Colonel said 'You both have a Flight to Jakarta and then on to the UK. Sam you will go to the Officers School at Camberley and assist the instructors in jungle warfare. Len you will go to the Commando school at Bickleigh, Devon and join the teaching staff there. It's been more than a pleasure to have fought with you both during this campaign and I wish you both all the luck in the world!.' They all stood, saluted and left. They both collected fourteen day leave passes from the clerk as they left the building.

Chapter 15

The flight to India was rough and uncomfortable as they were both sitting in the cargo hold. They changed planes and took off within four hours of touching down in India. They were on their way home stopping for refueling in Zurich. The Dakota touched down at Northolt Airport at 0900 hours on a cold English January morning. Both Sam and Len stood on the airfield apron waiting for their baggage to be off loaded. Two old khaki coloured humbers turned up,

'Major Lassiter?' a little voice chirped. 'Roger to that Corporal' Sam replied. 'Get in the Humber sir and I will collect your baggage. If Colours could take the other vehicle please.' said the Corporal.

After a salute and a bear hug both men settled down in their respective vehicles and with their baggage in the boot set off. Sergeant Jackson to King's Cross station for his trip home to Halifax and Sam en-route to the Officers School at Camberley. 'I'm Corporal Emilyn Jenkins and I'll be looking after you sir during your stay in Camberley.' 'The first thing I need to get sorted are my uniforms Corporal, my best blues and number 3's haven't been out of my wardrobe since 1942.' said Sam. 'I can attend to all that sir twenty four hours on Campus' the Corporal answered. 'Where are you from Corporal?' said Sam trying to make conversation during the one hour journey to the officers school. 'Port Talbot Sir' said Corporal Jenkins.

'Has very much changed at the Officers school during the last four years?' Sam asked, 'I've been here for two years and a lot of modernisation has occurred on Campus. A new accommodation block, new showers and what used to be the canteen has now been upgraded to a restaurant. You have been allocated a room in the new accommodation area sir.' said the Corporal.

They arrived just after 1030 and were checked in by the sentries guarding the entrance. The red and white barrier was lifted and the Humber passed through and then passed outside D block of the new building.

'Come on up with me' said Sam to Corporal Jenkins. 'Aye, aye sir!' Jenkins replied.

Sam placed his trunk on the bed and opened it. He sorted all his clothes that needed washing, hung up his best blues, number 3's and khaki battle dress. 'Can you get the washing sorted Corporal?' said Sam.

'It will be returned to you in the morning sir' said Jenkins who gathered up the dirty clothes and disappeared out of Sam's new quarters. Corporal Jenkins returned within twenty minutes and told Sam that his washing was sorted. 'These uniforms need cleaning and pressing Corporal.' said Sam removing the medal bars. 'Sir, you can call me Dai if you want to when no one else is around. If that's okay with you sir?' said the Corporal. 'Fine with me Dai. I'll probably need my best blues this weekend, so chop, chop with the cleaning Dai.' said Sam. Corporal Jenkins grabbed the two uniforms and was gone.

At the end of each accommodation block was a wash and ironing room, so Sam took his battle dress and his one remaining clean shirt to this area, heated up the iron and meticulously ironed his khaki shirt and his khaki battle dress. As he left the wash room Dai returned, off loaded all of Sam's washing and put them in a drier. 'I noticed your wings and your cross rifle's need a bit of work sir, I'll deal with that.' said Corporal Jenkins.

Sam left his batman in the wash room and returned to his room. He laid some newspaper over the shiny new table and laid out his webbing, both black and white. He polished the brass on each belt and worked the shine on the black webbing. He did the same in the white gear as far as the brasses were concerned and used "Blanko" to whiten up. He replaced the brasses on the belts and hung them on a hanger in his locker. He then polished his footwear, best drill boots, SV boots and two pairs of shoes, one black and one brown. He removed his white cap with the red band from its travelling bag, pressing it back into shape and cleaning the white and brushing the red. His final cleaning job was the brass RMs that he removed before sending his blues off for cleaning. He cleaned his green beret and white hat badges and replaced them back into place.

Corporal Jenkins poked his head into Sam's room and said 'Don't forget you need to be with Colonel Mike Samways at 1400 sir.' 'Roger to that Dai. I hope he doesn't mind seeing me in jungle greens.' said Sam,

'Nah he won't bother at all, he's a nice guy' replied Dai. 'I'll leave you now sir and chase up the washing' said Dai 'I'll catch up with you later Corporal.' Sam replied.

Sam took a shower and shaved off two days worth of growth and dressed for his rendezvous with Colonel Samways. He was dressed in combat gear, a jungle green flak jacket, jungle green denim trousers, black webbing, black SV boots, putee's and a green beret.

As he marched towards the C.O's office he looked out of place, seeing other officers decked out in best blues. He entered the office just outside the C.O's office and was ushered to a seat and told that the Colonel would see him shortly. After a couple of minutes a young handsome blond haired individual with new coloured pips on his shoulders appeared in the doorway of the C.O's office. 'Major Lassiter, welcome to my humble abode.' said the Colonel 'Sorry Sir I was taken aback a tad. I didn't expect you to be so young' said Sam feeling a little red under the collar. 'Me too' said the Colonel, giving Sam the once over. They both sat down opposite to one another. 'You are the first V.C that I have met Major and I regard it as an honour.' said Colonel Samways, 'Just being in the right place at the right time Colonel, with the best fighting men in the Commando's.' said Sam. 'I believe you have a two weeks leave pass Major. You are welcome to stay as long as you like here on campus.' he said. 'How old are you Major?' he continued, 'I turned twenty five last October sir.' said Sam. 'I have received notification today from the Department of Defence that as from today you have been promoted to Lieutenant Colonel,, he paused to see the effect that the news had on Major Lassiter. 'Welcome to the club Sam' said the Colonel with a handshake and a smile. Sam couldn't believe what had just happened. 'I don't believe it, somebody has got their knickers in a twist.' he said. 'I can't think of anyone more deserving this appointment' the Colonel said. 'You have ten days to prepare for your assignment and that is to take command of the Commando school at Bickley' the Colonel said, 'I would very much like to have Colour Sergeant Jackson at the posting with me Sir and two men from my old 'A' troop in Burma. They are Corporal T Morgan and Marine J Roberts, Sam replied. 'Colours will be joining you at Bickleigh on the 15 January. I will see if we can extract the two marines from Burma.' said Colonel Samways. 'Thank you sir' said a visibly shaken Sam. 'I still outrank you Colonel Lassiter, so let's go to the Officers mess, I think you need a drink.' said Samways.

Sam was still in a daze as they entered the mess 'Two double scotches barman.' said Colonel Samways. Sam sat down, his mind turning things over, it was hard to believe. A bloody Colonel and I'm still "Nawt but a kid" as Colours would say. Sam thanked the Colonel and left the mess to return to his room. Corporal Jenkins was sorting all Sam's recently washed and ironed clothing. 'You're not going to believe what happened today' said Sam, 'I'm a bloody Colonel!' 'Congratulations sir' said the Corporal. 'Can you get the required pips and crowns for a Lieutenant Colonel?' said Sam 'And get them sewn onto my uniforms when they arrive back from the cleaners?', 'Of course, sir.' said Jenkins.

Sam pulled out his 'Sam Brown' Officers highly polished shoulder belt, gave it a bit of a polish, paying attention to the brass buckles. Corporal Jenkins returned in twenty minutes with all the relevant pips and crowns to adorn Sam's uniforms. He produced two Lieutenant Colonel slip on insignia, undid the lapels on Sam's jungle green flak jacket and slid them onto the epaulets. 'I'll prepare the other uniforms myself tomorrow Colonel Sam.' said the Corporal.

Chapter 16

Sam, still dressed in his combat greens, went to the restaurant as soon as it opened at 1830 hours for an early dinner. The new restaurant was so much more up market. As Sam sat on his own, as near to the place where he sat four years ago when he met Trisha. Officers didn't need to queue they were waited on. A shy young lady arrived at his table and said 'What would you like Colonel, can I help you?' It was so strange to hear someone call him Colonel, it would take a bit of getting used to. 'Yes young lady, I'll have the pate followed by the lasagne please.'

'Very good, sir' she said adjusting his knife, fork and napkin. 'Excuse me asking young lady, but is Mrs. Jevons on duty tonight?' said Sam 'I would like to see her', 'I believe she is still in her office, sir, I'll check.' The young waitress lightly tapped on the door of Trisha's office and said 'Mrs J, there is a young, good looking Colonel in the restaurant and he said he would like a word with you.' 'Do you think he's going to complain Sally?' said Trisha Jevons. 'He is very polite and a really nice looking young man, very young to be a Colonel.' said the waitress. Both ladies entered the restaurant at the same time and Sally pointed into the direction of Sam's table. Trisha was a few feet away when Sam raised his head from the menu and said 'If you weren't a married woman, I'd ask you out for a date.' 'Sam, she said, tears formed in her eyes as she moved in close to the now standing Sam. Trisha gave Sam what must have been the longest hug of all time. Neither of them said anything they just melted in each others arms. Finally, Trisha sat down at Sam's table, tears flowing down her cheeks.

'Are you OK Mrs Jevons?' the little waitress said. 'I'm fine Sally, you can serve the other officers now.' Said Trisha. 'Well that Mr Jevons is a lucky guy, you are even more beautiful than you were when I took you to the dance four years ago.' Sam said. 'I can't believe that shy lieutenant I knew is now a Colonel' said Trisha. 'Neither can I' said Sam. They talked for half an hour catching up on all that had happened in the last four years. 'When I read in the paper that you had been awarded the Victoria Cross, I was both very proud of you, but also angry that you had taken so many chances', 'Let's not dwell on that' said Sam 'I'm just so pleased to find you so happy and content and congratulations on your promotion to supervisor.' Sam said. 'There's a dinner dance in the Officer's mess tomorrow. I will reserve a table for six' said Trisha. 'Six?' said Sam. 'David and me, Katherine and you and Lance and his fiancee, whose name I can't remember.' Trisha replied

The following day, the Saturday, Sam's blues were still not ready, so he decided to wear his khaki battle dress, with black webbing, black shoes and his green beret. As he approached the officers mess, he heard the music and the beat of a Glen Miller number Pennsylvania 65000 he recalled, being played by the Royal Signals dance band. He arrived 15 minutes after 2000 hours and made his way across the mess to a table where Trisha and her husband Trevor were chatting away with Katherine. Lance, as usual, quiet and on the edge of things holding hands with a pretty girl with an enormous rock on her finger. Her name was Yvonne, Sam was greeted by all at the table, it was good to see Lance and Katherine again after all those years.

Sam was the only officer in the mess dressed in khaki gear. All the other attendees were either in dress uniforms or in non-military type civvies. Sam looked splendid in his battle dress. His Royal Marines Commando flashes on each arm with a red dagger below them. His wings highlighted in a light shade of blue and his cross rifles recently touched up by Corporal Jenkins, boldly showing on his left sleeve. On his chest were four rows of medal bands sewed above his left breast pocket. The Victoria Cross, the DSO, the George Medal and various other less important medals.

There was so much to talk about, a lot of things had happened over the last four years. Lance stood up and said 'I'm off to the bar, is it the same again?, everybody chorused 'Yes.' 'Sam come with me and help with the carrying of drinks' said Lance. They got to the bar and Lance ordered the round of drinks.

'I'm getting married in June' said Lance 'And I want you to be my best man' he continued.

'It would be an honour, Captain' said Sam. 'We will be getting married in the local church in our village and the reception will be at Sunningdale Manor, my folks home. Best blues and white gear, sorry Sam.' said Lance. 'Looking forward to it.' said Sam

They returned to the table and dispensed the drinks. Trisha, Katherine and Yvonne were busily chatting away girls talk and Dave was circulating and with other non-military types. The band started playing a waltz. 'Come on Sam, let's dance, four years between dances has got to be some kind of record.' Trisha said.

Trisha and Sam stepped onto the dance floor and glided into the waltz. The dance floor was crowded, full of couples trying to avoid bumping into one another. Trisha pulled Sam into an archway that was dimly lit, just off the dancing area.

'I'm supposed to lead' said Sam.

Trisha stopped in her tracks held onto Sam, pulled him close and planted a long passionate kiss on his mouth, her tongue working overtime. 'I've been waiting to do that for four years and I'm glad I did it' she said. They returned to resume the waltz just in time before the end of the song. Trisha wiped the lipstick from Sam's mouth and he walked her back to the table. David returned to the table and gave his wife a quick kiss and sat down with the rest of the party. The band struck up with a romantic foxtrot. Katherine looked at Sam and said 'Fancy a smooch, Colonel?' 'Let's do it' said Sam. Neither Sam or Katherine could master the precise steps of the foxtrot, so they more or less shuffled along to the music. 'I think it's a good idea if you leave Camberley Sam.' She whispered 'She still loves you, you know!' sad Katherine.

'You are right again Katherine, the problem is I am also in love with her, but I would never step over the

line. She seems so happy and Trevor is a nice guy.'
Sam said.

The evening finished with all standing for the national
anthem. They said their goodbyes and made their way
to staff vehicles to take them to their various homes.
Sam retired to his room and looked around. Jenkins
had done a great job, the room was immaculate and in
his locker hanging was his blues all clean and pressed,
with the suitable Colonel insignia in place, He would
inquire whether he could take Corporal Jenkins with
him to Bickleigh.

On the last night of his stay in Camberwell, he was
sitting at his small table with the table light on putting
the final touches to program for the forthcoming week.
He would be driven to the Royal Marine barracks at
Lympstone to give a presentation to the Officers and
men. He had already written to the Colonel in charge
outlining his talk and suggested that it would make
a greater impact on the men if it was conducted on a
questions and answers format.

Chapter 17

He was packed and ready to go at 0800 hours the following morning, his battle dress and black gear beautifully prepared by Corporal Jenkins. He put down his pen at midnight having completed the fundamentals of his additional training ideas for the commando school and was ready to travel. He stripped to a pair of shorts and a t-shirt and climbed into bed, setting his alarm clock for 0600 hours in the morning.

He was quietly dozing off, when he heard a quiet tap on his door, 'Who is it?' said Sam. 'It's me, Trisha' a tiny voice replied. Sam opened the door and there she was shivering in the dim light. She pushed past him into the room and said 'Please don't think badly of me Sam, I had to see you one more time', 'What about Trevor?' said Sam. 'He is away for a couple of days on business.' added Trisha.

Sam wasn't sure how to react to this and sat down on his bed. Trisha standing in the dimly lit room took off her overcoat, dropped her skirt to reveal two beautifully shaped legs and the tinniest pair of white knickers Sam had ever seen. Then she slowly undid her blouse, button by button. All that was needed was a strippers musical accompaniment. She stood for a moment completely naked in front if Sam. Damn she was totally gorgeous, thought Sam. She moved to the other side of the bed and removed Sam's t-shirt and climbed into his bed. Sam stood up to remove his pants, they were bulging with a massive hard on. He hung his pants on the end of his penis and stood gazing at this beautiful woman in his bed.

'Nice clothes line Sam' said Trisha. She leaned over and they both started kissing each other, tongues going in and out like a fiddlers elbow. Sam was caressing her breasts and kissing her passionately, his hand wondering due south and he gently played with her soft pubic hair and her vagina, which was now very moist. She climbed on top of Sam and guided his now very erect member inside her and she rode him until they both climaxed and collapsed. After a prolonged hug, Trisha left the bed, dressed, planted a kiss on Sam and said 'Goodbye my love and take care of yourself.' and was gone.

Chapter 18

Sam rose at 0700 hours, washed and dressed and was standing outside his quarters at 0800 hours, still with a faint hint of Trisha's perfume lingering. Corporal Dai Jenkins arrived in the same humber staff car he had used to collect Sam from Northolt. He loaded his gear. Sam took one last look at Camberwell as Dai drove slowly through the campus. When they passed the staff restaurant, he saw Trisha standing alone, tears in her eyes and waving, 'Keep driving Corporal.' said Sam. Dai Jenkins eased the Humber out of the gate, hung a right and headed towards the A3. The journey was uneventful and Sam took time out to catch up on some sleep. He woke up just as Dai picked up the A303 at Andover. The English country side looked wonderful compared to the dense heavy jungle of Burma. 'Next town Exeter' said Dai 'Then we'll take take the B road into Lympstone.' Sam added.

He arrived at the Lympstone barracks three hours after leaving Camberley, Corporal Jenkins off loaded Sam's kit, said goodbye and saluted Colonel Sam Lassiter RM. 'Sir' a voice said 'I'm to look after you during your visit here Sir, I'm Marine Johnson.' he said. 'Drop my gear off in room 34 please Johnson' Sam said. 'Aye, aye sir' Johnson replied.

Sam went for a walk around the barracks and was amazed at the changes that had taken place in the last five years or so. The old Nissan huts were long gone, to be replaced with brick buildings with central heating, wash rooms and showers. A new vast drill shed had been built on the edge of the square, so that drill/ activities would not be interrupted due to inclement weather. The Tarzan assault course had been slightly modified only and that bloody wall was still in place.

He went to the officers' mess and met the camp C.O Colonel David Strange who introduced Sam to the camp Adjutant and various other officers in the mess. 'Lets take dinner Colonel' said Strange,

'Lovely.' said Sam who was feeling a bit peckish as he hadn't eaten since last evening. The officers' mess was a new building and supported by an excellent new kitchen facility. The tables, chairs, cutlery were all immaculate in typical marine style. On the wall dead centre was painted Royal Marine Badge with the motto *Per Mare, Per Terram (By Sea, By Land)* in bold print underneath it. On the remaining walls were pictures of all the Royal Marines that had been awarded the Victoria Cross. 'Those spaces there' said Strange pointing to a gap in the photo's 'Are reserved for you Colonel and Colour Sergeant Jackson'.

The following morning Sam sat on a chair in No1 blues. The photographer took pictures of Sam waist upwards and with his white cap alongside him at the table. He had help from Marine Johnson to put on his chest full of medals. He had no practice at this as it was the first time he had worn them. The photographer collected his lights, white umbrella and camera and left.

Sam went to the mess and had lunch and then made his way to the new cinema where he went to make his presentation. A table with three seats was on stage, just to the right of the screen. One seat was taken by General Farquason-Keith the second by the commanding officer Lympstone and Sam occupied the third chair. The cinema was packed with two hundred men, officers, NCO's, Marines and recruits. The General stood. 'Six years ago 626 squad had just commenced their twelve week training program and was their troop commander. Sergeant Crook who was their drill instructor brought this little guy, ten stone, wet through to my notice, he had potential leadership qualities. We followed his progress during his training. Top man in all the theory exercises, excellent on the parade ground, gear immaculate, marksman on both the rifle and Bren.'

'Sergeant Crook' yelled the C.O from the steps of his office 'you and recruit Lassiter to my office after the parade.' 'Aye, aye sir' said the Sergeant. '626 squad was dismissed and Sergeant Crook and Recruit Lassiter kept their appointment with me' the General continued. 'I asked recruit Lassiter if he would like to be fast tracked to be an officer. His reply I remember was yes as long as it was with the Royal Marines. The rest gentlemen is history.' he finished and sat down. The C.O them stood, switched on the microphone and said 'Gentlemen Lieutenant Colonel Sam Lassiter.' Sam rose from his seat and made his way to the dais where the overhead projector was situated. The whole audience stood up and applauded as Sam walked across the stage. When Sam put up his hand for the applause to stop he said in the microphone 'That was unexpected.'

He began his presentation. 'I'm not much of a talker, so I've put a bunch of photographs together for you to get some kind of idea what it's like to be a fighting man. I'll make comment throughout the screening and if you have any questions gentlemen leave them until the end and we'll have a questions and answers session.' Up on the screen the first photo was of A troop 44 commando in front of the Sergeants' mess. The mess was a bamboo hut lashed together and looked an eye sore, 'Just like your mess here, right Sergeant Crook' said Sam as he spotted the NCO trying to creep in his seat unnoticed. 'It's good to see you again Colours.' said Sam, Colour Sergeant Crook going a little red nodded.

He completed the picture show and amid more applause returned to his seat on the stage. 'Any questions for us?' the CO said.

A marine Captain stood and asked 'A question to Colonel Lassiter' he said 'How did you know how to fire a Lewis gun and how did you know how to dismantle a Howitzer?' he asked. Sam put one hand on the mic as it was passed along the table 'I had in A troop, probably the finest and smartest Royal Marine Sergeant in the far east. His name is Len Jackson and he was an engineer before he enlisted. We studied drawings of all the weapons, not only ours, but American and Japanese as well. By the time he had finished lecturing me for a period of six months, I could have achieved a degree at Cambridge or Oxford with the knowledge gained from my Colour Sergeant. Incidentally, Colour Sergeant Len Jackson as you know was awarded the Victoria Cross. He will be joining me at the commando school as an instructor' said Sam.

He was asked many questions on jungle fighting techniques and he verified the importance of fitness and the control of what you eat. Finally he said 'We will be introducing a lot of new ideas in jungle fighting at the commando school during the next few months and some of you guys will be there to benefit from these new findings.' he said. As he sat down he said 'Maybe we can find a few snakes for you to kill, cook and eat'. He sat down with a smile on his face. The C.O said that the presentation was now over and asked the Marines to return to their duties. Sam turned to the General and said 'Thanks for everything sir'.

'It's not a problem Colonel.' the General replied walking across the stage to the microphone. He switched it on and all the men stopped leaving the building.' Colour Sergeant Crook, report to the officers mess and if you have any trouble getting in, tell them you're with me'. Colours nodded and mouthed 'Aye, aye sir.'

The Generals entourage, together with Sam adjourned to the Officers mess. 'Stick the drinks on my tab young man' he said to the Marine barman. Very good sir' 'Two brandy's, large please' said the General Colours what's your poison?' he said seeing Colour Sergeant Crook emerging from the crowd. 'I'm not on duty Sir, so I'll take a whisky please' replied Colours. They all sat down at a large table near a window through which was a beautiful view across the river Exe. 'Colours come and sit alongside Colonel Lassiter and me' said the General. Sam began 'It's good to see you again Colours, what have you been up to for the past four years?' 'It's good to see you again too' said Colours 'Much of the same really Colonel, turning recruits into Royal Marines' said

Colours. 'Just as I left for commando school in '39, you were about to be married. Did that happen Colours, or did the bride to be have other ideas?' said Sam. 'Yes we did get married in '39 and we now have a two year old lad running and jumping all over us sir!' said Colours,

'That's great Colours, she's a lucky lady and thanks for the help regarding going to officer's school. I wouldn't have done it without the guidance from the General and yourself.' Said Sam.

'You painted a pretty picture on what it was like in Burma to the men an hour ago, but what was it really like Colonel?' said Colours. 'Fucking tough Colours, an un-officer type response I'm sorry, but it was not a nice place to fight.' Said Sam. 'I have put in place additional training programs for the commando school. A more in depth look at how the Japanese fight, how to combat disease and what to eat and what not to eat. It is very important to understand these things.' he concluded. 'Sounds pretty rough over there.' said Colours. 'As a bears arse.' said Sam. 'I saw so much cruelty by the Japanese and so much death. I really had to get out of there, but before I leave the corps, I intend to pass on as much of the knowledge I gained in Burma to the men when they come to Bickleigh.' said Sam. 'I think WW2 will be over this year, we are pushing hard in Europe, the Russians are running amok in the east, the combined forces in Burma have nearly pushed the Jap's into the Gulf of Bengal, the Yanks are steadily moving through the Philippines, although as usual they are throwing lots of men into the action and having a lot of casualties.' said the General. 'What are you going to do when it's all over Colonel?' said the General

'The VC could cause a problem with the powers that be using me for recruitment and me making speeches, I couldn't do that sir.' said Sam 'When we were in the early part of the Burma campaign, A troop sponsored a young Burmese lad, who showed immense promise in medicine, to travel to the USA and study to become a Doctor. He wrote to me last week and sent a cheque made out to Lieutenant Lassiter. The amount was much more than I originally gave him. I placed the cheque in an account at Camberley, I would deal with it later. He apparently had become very successful and has surgeries in Dos Angeles and New York. He specializes in plastic surgery and is amazed in what women will pay to get their breasts bigger, their tummies flat and their legs free from fat. His name is Li and he became a very good and trusted friend when I was in Burma.' said Sam 'He has invited me to go to LA and stay with him and his American wife in Santa Barbara when I leave the corps, I may just do that.' said Sam.

Chapter 19

After an hour of small talk Sam stood up and said 'I think I have a staff car and driver waiting for me gentlemen and I've got to get to my first command.' 'Good luck' the Colonel said and shook Sam by the hand. 'Thank you sir, for everything.' said Sam. He turned and faced Colour Sergeant Crook and said 'Thanks Colours, come over to Bickleigh for a visit' and after giving the man a hug, Sam turned and walked away to his staff car and instructed the driver to move out. As the old Humber drove out of the barracks at Lympstone the General turned and addressed the remaining officers and said 'Tough little bastard that Sam', 'And some' added Colour Sergeant Crook.

Sam arrived at the Royal Marine Commando School at Bickleigh in Devon some time after 1600 hours. The driver took Sam's bag to his quarters and returned to his vehicle, climbed in and started out on his return journey to Lympstone. Sam's new room was very grand and he thought to himself Jesus how the other half live. A writing table with a table lamp on it, a nice bed, radio and large wardrobe and drawers for his gear. He unpacked and sorted his gear away, hanging his best blues and battle dress in the wardrobe. He neatly folded his socks and underwear before placing them in the ample chest of drawers.

He wrote a note and pinned it on his door. It read: *Do not disturb, I will meet you all Monday next at 0800 hours. Please excuse me I'm really tired. Signed Lt. Colonel S. Lassiter.* He took off his clothes, fell on the bed and had a long, deep sleep. A knock on his door at 0900 hours woke him and he said 'Yes.'

'It's Marine Summers sir, I'm your new Batman here sir.' 'Give me ten minutes Summers and come back to my room' said Sam. 'Very good sir' said Marine Summers.

The new batman returned to Sam's room five minutes early in true marine fashion, knocked on Sam's door and waited. 'Come in Summers' said Sam, 'A couple of things I want you to do me Marine Summers'.

'If it's okay with you sir and we are out of earshot from other personnel, would you call me Sonny?' said his batman. Sonny it is' said Sam 'Two things. One give this note to Captains Watts and Sterling. and two,' he said picking up a black bag 'Let's get some washing and ironing done for me please.'

'No probs, sir' said Sonny and left Sam's quarters.

The note to Watt's was brief, meet me together with Captain Sterling and the two tenants whose names I have forgotten in the officers mess at 1400 hours. Dress informally, it's Saturday. Added Sam to the note.

He sat down at his desk and wrote a long letter to Dr. Li congratulating him on the wonderful progress he had made and ended the letter saying that he may take him up on the offer he made by joining him in

California. He stamped and addressed the envelope and started to write to Katherine. It was basically saying that he had arrived at the commando school, but was still a little nervous taking on his first command. He finished by saying that he was looking forward to seeing her again in April at Lance's wedding. He placed the stamped envelope in a file labeled post to go. He would put Sonny in the picture later.

He washed and changed into a jungle green jacket, khaki shirt and fatigues and made his way over towards the officer's mess. Before he left Camberley, Sam had paid a visit to the archive library to find out more on the history of the base at Bickleigh. A quiet young lady talking in a whisper said: 'This will do nicely, sir' and she produced an old battered hard back entitled Commando School, by Colonel John Palmer. She then managed to find a full scale drawing of the base, retired to the dark room and produced a copy for Sam.

'Good work young lady. I'll return the book to you in the morning.' said Sam. 'Very good, sir' said the librarian.

It was 0900 hours as Sam set off to the mess. The base was very quiet this Sunday morning, only a few men around for Sam to acknowledge with a salute. He detoured and entered the NAFFI where an old three badger was cleaning the floor facing away from Sam and he said: 'Can I help you mate?', 'Yes mate, Is the boss of this place around?' asked Sam with a smile on his face. The old three badger turned towards Sam and said 'Jesus Christ, I'm really sorry sir', 'Not a problem' said Sam 'Is the boss about?' 'I'll fetch him sir. Jesus' He muttered as he fled away.

'Good Morning sir. I'm Doris Lawson, the boss around here.' 'Nice to meet you Doris, I'm Sam Lassiter, the boss of the Base.'

They both had a little laugh about this. Sam dived into his brief case and pulled out a drawing of the NAFFI building, together with a sketch pad.

'The training program starts on April 1st, so what I'm going to propose to you, if you agree, needs to be completed quickly.' he said. 'This is what I want you to put to your superior Doris' Sam began and then referred to his drawing of the NAFFI layout. 'I want a stage here' he said drawing a line across one end of the floor plan, 'Steps on each side of the stage, coming back towards the bar. I want two snooker tables, a scoreboard and cue rack adjacent to each table and two dart boards.' he continued 'I would also like a taut, rugged carpet laid in this area, I'll leave the colour to you.' he said. 'Half way back towards the bar an aluminum strip will be placed across the room and from the strip to the bar a tough, hardened lino will be fitted. This will separate the playing area from the dining area. The bar looks good and will remain in tact.' He said. 'One more thing Doris, is that if you require any modernization in the kitchen, the Royal Marines will come up with half the money as they will for alterations to the NAFFI. Get your man in here and put the plan to him. Please advise my office when he is likely to appear. Many thanks Doris.' he said and left the building.

His next port of call was the Sergeants and Junior NCO's mess. It was absolutely pristine as Sam entered. Again two civvies along with a red faced Sergeant were busy cleaning the place. 'You'll polish the place away,

Sergeant' said Sam. 'I've been trying for years sir. Sergeant Bill Clarke ex 44 commando Sir. Your old unit too I believe?' said the Sergeant. 'Who's in charge of this place, Sergeant?' asked Sam.

'That would be me, sir' replied the Sergeant. 'Come here and have a look at this' said Sam pulling a plan out of his brief case and spreading it flat on a table.

'My proposal is to lose the Sergeants mess and put the NCO's in together with the officers and call it The Mess' said Sam. 'And' he continued 'You will be in charge Sergeant Clarke' said Sam. 'So, you could be in charge of The Mess or be IC for the cinema which I intend to change this into' said Sam referring to his plan 'Take a look at this Sarge" he said 'A stage, a screen, one hundred and twenty fold up seats and hard wearing carpets, an exit each side of the building, a projector and a projection room. The cost I've estimated at is £4,000. What do you think Sarge'?' he said finally. 'I would like to give the cinema a go, sir' said Sergeant Clarke. 'You have the appointment Sarge" said Sam. 'Come to my office in the morning at say 1100 hours and I will give you £500 for you to purchase the hundred and twenty theatre seats that were saved from a bomb raid made by the Germans. They are said to be in good condition. When you get the cheque take two three tonne trucks to a storage depot on Croydon airfield and collect the seats.' Said Sam. 'Aye, aye, sir.' said the Sergeant.

His final call was to the Officers Mess, a huge beautifully kept building on the edge of the parade ground.

The four officers sat down at a table near the window and looked at Sam to start the meeting. 'First of all, let me get to know you better,' said Sam 'Let's go round the table and you guys tell me who you are and what your main function is at the base.' he continued 'I believe you are aware of my past, but for the record I am Lieutenant Colonel Samuel Lassiter ex 44 commando'. 'Captain Smithers sir. I look after and assist in lectures on tactics, weapons and street fighting.' he said. 'Captain Whiting sir. I do more or less the same as Captain Smithers, but I do assist in unarmed combat and physical fitness.' 'Lieutenant Powell sir. Mainly running the Tarzan Course and the speed and route marches along with NCO instructors.' 'Paignter, the same as Lieutenant Powell sir. Especially when we have more than one squad in from Lympstone.'

'Excellent' said Sam."

'Down to business then, I have £15,000 to spend donated by a dear Doctor friend of mine, who I met during the Burma campaign' he continued 'I don't think you are going to like what I have to say, but here goes' Sam said. 'When the recruits arrive from Lympstone, we drive them hard and there will be a few drop outs on the way. They have two options at the moment. Go down the village for a pint or train to Exeter for an expensive night out!' Sam continued, 'So I have put the following arrangements in place. One – will upgrade the NAFFI at a cost of around £4,000 of which we will be paying half. The other half will hopefully be paid by the NAFFI people. Go along and see Doris who will show you the plans on what we want to do.' said Sam. 'Two – we will convert both the Sergeant's and NCO's mess into a cinema with a hundred and twenty seats. This is a major operation and is left in the capable hands of Sargent Clarke. You, Captain Smithers being the senior officer here will assist Clarke and generally keep an eye on things as this will be the most expensive project' continued Sam. 'This is the bit that you're not going to like, but it will happen nevertheless. The Officers Mess is a beautiful building inside and out, but far too big and grand for just five officers and the occasional visiting officer and is completely not viable cash wise. So, I've decided for the officers and the NCO's to merge and dropping the word officers it will now be known as The Mess.' He concluded, 'If you don't like what you have heard here, don't go running off at the mouth to the powers that be, come and see me face to face and we'll discuss it' said Sam 'By carrying out these projects it will establish two things: A better working relationship between officers and NCO's and an improvement in the recruits down time, which I believe will benefit the whole situation.' Sam said breathing a sigh of relief.

Chapter 20

Sam stood and fished out four packages containing the additional training packages he and Len had put together during the last two weeks. 'Colour Sergeant Len Jackson VC will be joining us tomorrow and any questions on the new format will be discussed then. So, gentlemen we will meet tomorrow, Perhaps Lieutenant Powell, you can arrange lunch for six?' said Sam finally, packed his brief case and left the building. That will give them something to think about, thought Sam.

Sam returned to his quarters and made a call to the General on his private line. 'General Farquason-Keith residence. Who's calling please?' 'Colonel Lassiter' replied Sam. 'I'll put you through sir, hold on please.' 'Hello young Sam and how the devil are you?' said a booming voice. 'I'm good sir. Sorry to bother you on the Sabbath sir, but you should know I've put some plans in place to modernize Bickleigh and I'm not sure of the reaction yet' said Sam 'There may be some crass comments flying around' said Sam.

'Have you used the money your Doctor friend gave you?' said the General. 'Yes sir. I have told Doc Li what I'm going to do with his donation and he is very happy.' Said Sam 'Excellent my boy. I'll be popping over to see you when all the mods have been completed.

Make sure the new mess is well stocked with Brandy' said the General. 'I'll look forward to seeing you Sir.' said Sam and replaced the phone in its cradle.

The next day, the Monday, was a busy one. Sam went to the Lloyds Bank in Exeter and got the money from Doctor Li transferred from Camberley, received a cheque for £500 and returned to base. He gave the cheque to Sargent Clarke and told him to get on the road to Croydon as soon as possible. The head honcho from the NAFFI turned up and together with Doris agreed to pay half of the NAFFI modifications. The General sent a Captain Myers from the Royal Engineers, who would supervise the contractors to put together the cinema and NAFFI projects.

Colour Sergeant Jackson arrived and went straight to his quarters, had a quick wash and returned to Sam's office. 'Good to see you Colours' said Sam. 'Good to see you' replied Colours. 'Take a peek at what I've prepared.' said Sam.

The meeting between Len and the NCO instructors went really well and it became obvious that a good working relationship was being established. Progress on the three projects was going well. The NAFFI alterations were more or less finished, all that needed doing was to get professional help to level off both the new snooker tables. Sam was most pleased with the progress on the Sargent's mess conversion to a cinema. The stage was finished, together with a screen projector in front of the already finished screen. The seats were fantastic in a dark coloured crimson in banks of six and stretching back eight rows either side of a central aisle.

Dust covers protected them whist the brickwork was taken out to prepare for the two exit doors. All that was left to do was installing an electric motor to open and close the curtains, emergency lighting each side of the cinema and the making of the curtains themselves. Sam made a special effort to say a well done to Sergeant Clarke.

The snooker table in the old Sergeants mess was transported over to the new combined officers and NCO's mess.

Chapter 21

A letter arrived the next day from Sir Keith Templeton requesting that Colonel Samuel Lassiter report to Sunningdale Manor on Friday 4th March to attend a marriage rehearsal for his son Lancelot. Sam replied confirming that he would be there, he had booked a room at the Officers school in Camberley in case he was not invited to stay at Sunningdale Manor. Sam got together with Sonny to work on his gear to ensure it was picture perfect for the wedding.

In between organising the training and building projects, Sam found time to take a little break in the mess. He sat drinking coffee and scanning the local newspaper. He was looking in the for sale section and spotted an MG-TF sports car for sale, British racing green, 1500 cc, soft top and in mint condition. He called the barman 'Freddie get me a telephone please.' The orderly ran the line across the room and placed the phone in front of Sam. 'Thanks Freddie' said Sam and dialed the number at the foot of the ad. 'I'm enquiring after the MG, is it sold yet sir?' asked Sam. 'I've had a lot of interest, but it's still here' came the reply. 'Don't sell it please until I've seen it please.' said Sam. 'You have my word on that young man, when will you be here?' 'Within the hour' said Sam 'Freddie, get me a pool car and a driver please, my office in 5 minutes' 'Aye, aye sir' said the bar keeper.

Sam and his driver were on their way to a place just to the north of Exeter. He stopped at the bank and took out £500. When he saw the beautiful MG he fell in love with it straight away, TF. series, even the number plate which read MAR 44. He agreed a price of £450, told his driver to return to base. Sam boarded the British racing green MG started it and took off at a rate of knots up the guys driveway. When he reached the open road he gunned it and took it up to seventy miles per hour. He was flying and he loved it.

He drove through the main gate at Bickleigh and went straight to the depot garage and car pool. 'What a little beauty' said a waiting motor mechanic. 'I'd love to have a go at tuning it Colonel' he continued.

'The job is yours Corporal. Make it fly' said Sam as he left for his quarters.

The big wedding was at Sunningdale this Saturday. A rehearsal was set up for this Friday. Sam departed Bickley on the Thursday morning in his newly tuned MG-TF. His number 1 best blues uniform in a coverall and his travel bag, neatly packed by Sonny, stored in the MG's little boot.

Chapter 22

Sam arrived at the gate outside Sunningdale Manor, parked the MG and strolled over to the gate house. He was met half way by an old guy in a long grey cot and top hat. 'Good morning. I'm Colonel Lassiter. I'm here for the wedding.' said Sam. 'And good morning to you sir' said the old fellow checking his list. 'Ah there you are' he said making a tick alongside Sam's name. As the old guy walked towards the gate he passed close to the MG which was idling at around eight hundred revs per minute. 'That motor has been set up nicely' he said 'Yes it is, it was breathed on by a former mechanic, who used to tune motors at Brooklands before the war. He is at present a Sergeant in my transport pool at Bickleigh.' said Sam. 'I used to race at Brooklands before the war, so I know the sound of a nicely tuned motor.' he said opening the two huge wrought iron gates. As Sam drove through the gates he said 'What's your name?'

'Carter sir, Jim Carter' he answered 'If I have time tomorrow I'll pop by and let you give her a go.' said Sam patting the dashboard of the TF. He drove through the gates and throttled back to thirty miles per hour along the four hundred yard drive to the manor, the drive was a smooth surface and lined either side by trees.

He reached the main entrance of the manor and saw another old-dish gentleman in a morning suit waiting for him at the foot of several steps leading up to the manor entrance. 'Good morning young man, I'm Simpson. May I take your baggage?' he said, Sam got out of the car, popped the boot and gave Simpson his case and uniform which was on a hanger and inside a protective holdall. 'I'll keep my hat Simpson. I don't want it crushed or damaged and you have enough to carry.' said Sam.

As Simpson plodded along towards the house Sam, turning to get back into his car, stopped and turned to face the steps. 'Hello Colonel Samuel Lassiter' Katherine said. 'Hello Lieutenant Katherine Templeton' replied Sam. She turned towards Simpson and inquired 'Are you okay with that load Simpson?' 'Yes mistress Kate, I'm fine' he replied.

She was dressed in beige coloured riding britches, riding boots, a white blouse and a pea green chiffon scarf tied behind her neck to secure her ponytail. She skipped down the steps, her ample breasts going all over the place under her blouse, it was obvious she wasn't wearing a bra. She went around to the passenger's side of the MG, peeled back the tone au cover and just about got her long legs into the car.

'Drive on McDuff and turn right at the end if the building' she said. 'Yes mistress Kate' Sam cheekily replied.

He roared the MG into life and took off along the front of the building. He turned right at the end and headed for the rear of the massive house. They reached a paddock area and slowed down. On the right were six stables, four of them occupied. Opposite the stables there was room for six cars to park under the car port. 'Stick it in the car port there' said Katherine pointing to a vacant space. Sam parked the TF, zipped up the tone au- cover and took his bagged hat from the boot. They both wandered across to the stables and Katherine introduced him to Soloman, a beautiful black stallion.

'He's my horse and he's worth a few bob' said Katherine 'We hire him out as a stud' she continued. They looked in on all the stables and Katherine gave him a short history of all the horses. They arrived at the last stable and Katherine said 'I've got something to show you, come in.' She stood aside as Sam went past her into the stable. It was a store full of clean hay with new window letting in minimal light. Katherine turned and placed the wooden door bar in place and walked towards the window.

'Take your jacket off Sam and relax.' she said. She took off her boots and riding britches to reveal the tiniest pair of white silk panties Sam had ever seen. She then slowly undid every button of her blouse, exposing two well rounded breasts. She walked over to the hay in the floor and lay down on her side, supporting herself on one elbow. Sam was watching and he was very conscious of having a huge hard on and tried to tuck it up, so it wouldn't be so apparent. 'I see you are pleased to see me' sad Katherine.

Sam removed his shirt and lay down beside her. He started to gently kiss her. Katherine was equally as good a kisser as Sam was. She had what Sam called a busy tongue. Sam's right hand caressed her breasts, while Katherine maneuvered her left hand and grabbed Sam's penis. 'Jesus Sam. What you got there a baseball bat?' she said, 'I'm sorry Katherine. A bloody Jap' shot three inches of my dick off and left me with a seven inch stump!' he teased. 'Yeah right' Katherine giggled.

Sam moved his lips from her mouth and made his way down south, cupping each breast and showering them with kisses and giving each nipple his undivided attention. He continued south passed her naval and buried his tongue in her sparse blond pubic hair. He parted the lips of her sex and located her clitoris with the tip of his tongue and began to gently tease it. This drove Katherine into ecstasy and before long she had one of many orgasms. Sam returned to face Katherine and said 'You okay?' 'Wonderful!' said Katherine. She rose from the prone position and straddled Sam, easing his erect penis inside herself. It was so smooth thought Sam like being massaged by a length of silk. Sam was not a good lover and often suffered from premature ejaculation. This time, however, he was determined to try and hold back. The trick was to think about boring things like crochet or bird watching someone had told him. Well it worked, after twenty minutes or so, Katharine's movement started to accelerate and she was bobbing up and down like a fiddlers elbow. They climaxed more or less together in a magical moment, then hugged each other afterwards.

'We had better get back to the house' said Katherine 'And by the way, don't worry about me getting pregnant, it can't happen.'

They both dressed quietly. Sam retrieved his hat, put some straw in it and placed it on his head and looked at Katherine. 'I always told you I was a country bumpkin.' he said. They both laughed, left the stable and returned to the house. They were greeted by Simpson, who informed them that tea and biscuits would be served in the parlor at 4pm. 'I'll show the Colonel to his room.' said Katherine.

She left him outside his room in the west wing and said that she would see him at 4pm and to dress informally. Sam said goodbye, stripped to his underwear, set his alarm clock for 3pm and slid into bed for a power nap.

Chapter 23

Right on cue the alarm sounded at 3pm, Sam took a shower, shaved and put on a clean shirt and trousers, brown shoes and a white cricket sweater trimmed in blue. He reached the entrance to the parlour at the same time as Katherine. She linked arms with Sam and they entered the room together.

'Daddy' Katherine called 'This is Colonel Sam Lassiter, Royal Marines, Lance's best man'.

Sir Keith Templeton turned and beamed a smile and said 'Colonel, I've heard so much abound you from both my son and daughter, it's so nice to meet you at last.' 'It's a pleasure to meet you too sir' said Sam

They shook hands and Sir Keith went on to say 'This is my wife Janet, she more or less runs the place you know.' Janet Templeton was the most beautiful women Sam had ever seen, blonde, petite and a face and body most women would die for. 'He's exaggerating again Colonel' she said smiling. Lady Janet Templeton oozed class in every way, the way she looked, dressed and spoke. 'Do you like art, Colonel?' she said looking at Sam. 'Very much so. Although I prefer the impressionists, Manet, Monet, Gaugin, Degas and the like' said Sam 'And please call me Sam.' he added. 'Excellent and you must call me Janet.' she replied. 'I'm sorry Ma'am, but it will always be Ma'am. I've been checking up on you and the work you have been doing with the refugees in London. If you were a man Ma'am you would have been knighted by now.' Said Sam. 'You are very kind Sam' she answered. 'Has my daughter shown you around the place yet Sam?' Lady Templeton queried. 'The outside only Ma'am.' said Sam. 'I want you to come with me to see what I've been up to in the long room'. 'Oh, pardon Ma'am I've just remembered, I need to ask you something' said Sam 'Your man Carter, at the front gate, is he working tomorrow?' Sam asked.

'I've given him half a day off as he will be working over the weekend, what with the wedding and all' she said 'Is there any way of contacting him Lady T?' Sam asked.

'Yes, any black phone. They are dotted around the place, dial 223' Lady Templeton said. 'A moment please Ma'am.' Said Sam picking up the nearest phone and dialing 223. 'Main gate, Carter here' 'Jim, it's Sam Lassiter. The guy with the little MG.' said Sam. 'How would you like to give her a burst tomorrow? Say about twelve noon?' 'I would love to sir' Carter replied. 'Twelve noon it is then Jim.' said Sam replacing the phone in its holder.

Lady Templeton cast a curious eye at Sam, but said nothing. 'Jim Carter your gate man used to race cars at Brooklands before the war and he told me yesterday that he would love to give my MG a bit of a clear out.' Said Sam 'What a nice thing to do Sam' replied Lady T. 'Lancelot you'll have to wait a bit longer for your best man to join you' she called out 'I'm taking him to the long room.' 'Okay Mother, don't be running off with him' said Lance. Sam raised his arm to Lady Janet and she obliged by placing her hand gently on top of the arm he offered and they both proceeded towards the long room, Sam taking tiny steps to ensure he kept in pace with the tiny Lady T. 'I'm turning the long room into a gallery, it's slow progress, but I'm winning.' she continued.

The room was newly decorated in a shade of cream with the purple drapes over the windows.

'I like the décor' said Sam. As they walked through the long room Lady T pointed out a river scene by Manet, a ballet picture by La Trec and several Rubens. 'So far, so good' she said 'I'm going to Sotherby's next week to see if I can add to the collection'. 'Don't buy any more Rubens, his women frighten me to death!' he joked. 'They are big girls' she said. 'I will be leaving the corps when this thing is over Ma'am and I shall be going across the pond to the United States. They have a few good up and coming painters at the moment and if I see something special I'll buy it and ship it over to you.' said Sam.

'Being such a nice, quiet young man, how on earth did you manage to get a Victoria Cross?' asked Lady Janet. 'I was in the right place, at the right time. I had a lot of good fortune and I was very angry' said Sam, as they left the long room and joined the main party in the parlour. 'Go and do your best man duties Sam. We'll talk again before you leave.' Said Lady T. 'We will Ma'am' said Sam, moving off to meet Lance and his Royal Engineer buddies.

Lance had certainly loosened up as he had got a little older and it was good to see. He was easily pushed around in his younger days. 'Good to see you buddy' said Sam 'Good to see you too, Sam' said Lance dispensing with the handshake and giving Sam a huge bear hug instead.

Chapter 24

The following morning all the principles for the wedding were ferried to the little church in the village. The bride and groom, Sir Keith and Lady Templeton. The two tiny bridesmaids together with their parents, the maid of honour and the best man.

The six Royal Engineers who were to act as the guard of honour were also present dressed in civvies and carrying there dress swords. The rehearsal was carried out by a plump happy faced little guy and it went without a hitch, everybody knowing where to stand and what to say. Sam took his leave and went directly to the manor main gate and located Jim Carter, vacated the MG driver's seat and offered it to Jim.

Jim Carter was an excellent driver and gave the MG a good clear out. 'Did you enjoy that Jim' said Sam, 'It brought back a lot of memories, thank you so much Sam'.

It was a perfect early spring April day for the wedding, brilliant sunshine and a deep blue sky. The whole wedding went like clockwork, all the main participants were taken to the church in Bentleys and Rolls Royce's. Lance and Sam arrived at the church that was already filling up, with two Royal Engineer officers guiding the attendees to the appropriate sides of the church.

Sam and Lance walked slowly down the center aisle, Lance stopping to chat with a few people before taking a seat at the front pew, and along with Sam waited for the bride. Outside the church the little bridesmaids and the maid of honour waited for the-bride to arrive. Then the first minor problem occurred, little Jenny Carpenter said in a voice a little above a whisper, 'Auntie Kate, I need a wee'. Katherine swung into action, taking the little girl's hand and leading her around the corner of the church to a large bush behind the vestry. The little girl did the business, Katherine tidied her up and they both returned to the entrance of the church just in time to greet the bride and her father. Katherine helped the bride out of the Rolls, making sure the ten foot long train didn't get dirty or damaged. She told the two little bridesmaids to hold on tight to the train as the stood poised ready for the big entrance.

The first chord of the wedding march rang out and the wedding party made their way along the centre aisle towards the waiting groom and best man. The service went like clockwork and after they were pronounced man and wife, Lance and his new bride walked slowly back down the centre aisle smiling and waving to friends. When the photographs were finished, the photographer gave Sam the nod.

Sam raised his voice and said, 'Everybody, can you please let the bride and groom get back to the Manor so that they can greet you when you arrive, thank you.' Lance and his bride set off for the Manor, the rest of the guests chatted to each other on the way to their cars and left for Sunningdale. Sam did a final check and satisfied that all was in order was last to leave in the one solitary Bentley. When Sam arrived at the manor he went directly to the top table and sat down next to the brides mother.

The meal over, it was time for the speeches, something that Sam was not looking forward to, all the rehearsing he had done completely forgotten. As he rose to speak the room went completely silent, which made Sam even more nervous. 'Can one of you little ones yell or something and make a little noise, the silence is killing me', he said. After some jibes from the Royal Engineer Officers, Sam felt more at ease.

'Picture if you will a cold December night in a dingy railway station cafeteria in Camberley. I ordered a cup of tea and a bacon sandwich from a lady called Mabel 'Here's your tea luv', I'll bring your sarnie' over' she said. I sat down opposite a long legged fellow who was eating a salad sandwich and was nursing a cup of coffee', Sam continued, 'I called over to him Sam Lassiter, Royal Marines', Lance Templeton Royal Engineers'. He replied 'I'm here for the officers course at WOSB Camberley', he said.

'I said so am I, stood and crossed over to his table and shook his hand'. Sam went on to say, 'We both settled down to finish our food with not to much conversation, something I would get used to during the next few weeks, Lance being a noisy and loud person'. A ripple of laughter around the room and a grin from Lance.

Two yobs entered the cafeteria went straight up to Lance and said 'lets have your money rich boy' 'I looked at Lance and he didn't budge,' 'I'm afraid that's a "no no" young man' and continued to sip his coffee, The biggest of the two thugs pulled a knife and waved it under Lance's nose. He still didn't move, looked at me and winked and slapped the guy across the face.'

'I joined in and within a half minute both men were doubled up on the floor cupping there wedding tackle. Lance walked over to the counter and said very quietly and in meticulous English. 'Mabel I think you should call the police and the ambulance service so that we can rid ourselves of these cretins', He sat down and turned towards me and said 'Now then Sam where were we. 'I'm used to violence but Lance isn't, but the way he conducted himself that day I will always remember.'

After a short while Lance turned to me and said, 'You're a violent bugger Sam' I looked at him and said, 'You amaze me Lance, no fear when you were threatened with a knife, not one moment of fear. I'll probably get a few boos from the Engineer's present, but Sam you would have made a fine Marine. 'I new from that moment that Lance would be my best friend and it's an honour to be here and asked to be his best man,' 'So the plan was put in place Lance would take care of the academic bits and bobs and I would take care of the hands on stuff. It worked and we both flew through Officer's School.'

'Before we toast the bride and groom I have a question to ask you Lance, was it you who hung the Sergeant Majors "long johns" on the parade ground flagpole?'

'I plead the 5th Amendment' said Lance.

'Finally I would like to wish my best friend and his lovely wife all the happiness in the world and a long and loving relationship'. 'The 'Bride and Groom" Sam sat down to a generous round of applause.

After a few more speeches Lance stood up and thanked everyone for coming and many thanks for the lovely presents. It was short and sweet and beautifully delivered. When all the speeches were finished and the food consumed Sam rose to his feet and said,

'If you would all please retire to your rooms or hotels please and you ladies make yourselves even more beautiful for tonight's ball here in the Long Room, 7.30 don't be late. If you would like to look around the Manor especially Lady Janet's Gallery, please do so.' Sam retired to his room on the West Wing took off his clothes, set the alarm for 6pm and went to sleep.

The alarm woke him at 6pm, he showered, shaved and put on clean underwear. He dressed for the first time in full Officers Evening ware which consisted of black shoes and socks, navy blue trousers with a red stripe, a brilliant red waistcoat length jacket. Finally he pinned on his chest full of mini medals, did a check in the full length mirror. He put on his white cap with a red band and was good to go.

The Long Room was almost packed when he arrived, so he quickly made his way to his designated area on the Top Table. The meal was wonderful and the service excellent, as the meal progressed to the desert course Sam clicked on the mic and stood up. 'Sorry to interrupt folks but as you can see we have some very valuable paintings in here and we would ask you please not to smoke in this area, a painting with a delicate nicotine sky is not so good, so anywhere else in the

Manor is good, thank you so much, we must look after Mr. Degas and Mr. Monet.' Nods of approval all around the Long Room were noticed by Sam and he turned to the beautiful Lady Janet Templeton and said, 'I think they got the message Ma'am.'

'If not I'll give them a little tickle with this Ma'am', he said spinning a steak knife on it's pointed end.

Lady Janet looked a little worried. 'Only kidding Ma'am' said Sam with a laugh.

Katherine approached him and said, 'Lets circulate Sam, you take the right and I'll take the left.' Half way round the Long Room he came to the table where Trevor and Trisha were sitting in deep conversation with the Minister who conducted the wedding service. 'Good to see you Sam' they both chorused.

'It's great to see you guys again' said Sam.

As Sam moved away from their table he turned and said, 'Save a dance for me Mrs. Jevons'. Sam carried out his best man duties to the full, dancing with the bride, Katherine, the two little bridesmaids and both mothers of the bride and groom. He sat down around 10.30. absolutely knackered 'Want to dance, sailor?' she said. He didn't need to look who asked the question, It felt good to feel her close again, he wondered if he would ever get her out of his system. 'I'm leaving the Corps when the war is finally over', said Sam

'It's good for you to get away from all that killing Sam', Trisha said, 'I'm going over to the States to meet up with a friend of mine, he's from Burma but has now settled in Santa Barbara, I'll just take it nice and easy and see what happens next', said Sam.

'That sounds great, but don't forget to write to me', she said. 'I'll write' Sam answered. The band finished the waltz and started to play a "Boogie. Woogie" 'Too quick for me, I must be getting old', said Sam.

They both laughed as Sam led her back to her table, held her seat for her as she sat down next to her husband Trevor. Sam saw Lance and his new bride to their room and then returned to the dance. Only a few people were dancing. Most of the guests were on the move saying their goodbyes. 'Sam said his good nights to Sir Keith and Lady Janet and moved over to Katherine and said. 'You completely knackered me yesterday, but if you would like a kiss and a cuddle-and a nice kip, you are welcome to my boudoir' said Sam. Katherine turned away from him smiled and said 'I'll be with you within the hour "stud"' she said,

Katherine drifted away to talk to a couple of Royal Engineer Officers. Sam went to his room stripped off and hung up his dress uniform and climbed into bed, making a point of not locking the door. About 12.30 he felt a warm body move in beside him, he took her into his arms and they embraced, a little kiss and they went to sleep.

Sam rose early in the morning leaving Katherine who was in a deep sleep. He had a couple of jobs to do to complete his best man duties. One was to ensure that the bride and groom were up and ready in plenty of time to meet there train departure time and to supervise getting their luggage stowed away in the Rolls.

These tasks duly completed he said his goodbyes to Sir Keith and Lady Janet and jogged to the carport to pick up the MG.

It was a nice sunny morning so Sam decided to drop the soft top. The MG came to life and he gently eased away from the waving Sir and Lady Templeton. He stopped at the gate to say goodbye to Jim the gate man, drove out the gate and turned left towards the A3 and A303 to Exeter. He made good time and after reaching Exeter took the B road to Bickleigh. A new sign greeted him just alongside the guard house, it read Royal Marines Commando School, Bickleigh Depot. The text surrounded a Royal Marine cap badge. Sam went directly to his room dropped off his luggage and marched across the parade ground to his office. Squad numbers 650 and 651 were arriving tomorrow and he needed to work on his welcome speech.

Captain Melville knocked and entered Sam's office. How are the modifications going Colin?', he said, 'Excellent sir, the new mess is completed and the alterations to the NAFFI. The final touches are being made to the new cinema, as we speak'. 'Excellent, lets go take a look. Sam was more that satisfied with what he saw and said. 'Well done Colin good job'. 'I'm going to my room Captain to finish off my welcome talk for the new squads coming in tomorrow' 'Very good sir', said Captain Melville.

At 10am the following morning, squads 650 and 651 arrived and were inspected and Sam liked what he saw. 'Dismiss the men Colours' he said, 'I want them assembled in the new cinema at 1400 hours, that will give them time for something to eat', 'Aye aye sir' replied the Colour Sergeant. At 1400 hours all the new intake were assembled in the cinema. On the stage sat the three officers, Colour Sergeant Jackson and Sam, a microphone was placed in the centre of the table. Sam grabbed the mic. 'Good morning gentlemen, welcome to Commando school, you all think that you are really fit after your initial training at Lympstone, forget it, you're not. You'll have aches and pains from muscles you never thought you had', said Sam

'Your Troop Commander is Captain Melville' said Sam pointing in the general direction of the table 'And Lt. James will be with 650 and Lt Wilson be with 651. The Colour Sergeant is Len Jackson VC and what he doesn't know about weapons and how to use them can be written on a postage stamp'. 'These gentlemen will be looking after you for the next 8 weeks, at which time you can throw away your Blue Berets and proudly wear a Green one, good luck gentlemen', said Sam sitting down. The Captain stood and said' You can see that we have a beautiful cinema here, an excellent canteen and a newly upgraded NAFFI, I expect you to respect these new facilities and keep them in pristine condition'. 'OK, your training starts in the morning at 0800 hours, your instructors will be taking you on a gentle bedding in 5 mile run'.

The following morning all the new intake were assembled and ready to go, all dressed in tee shirts and shorts. What they didn't expect was Colonel Sam Lassiter and Colour Sergeant Len Jackson, Captain Melville and the two Lieutenants joining them for the run.

For the next few weeks the new training schedule was working well and as yet no drop outs from either squad Sam assembled both squads after a successful trouble free "Tarzan Course" run and said,

'There has never been a squad that has passed through Bickleigh where every member of the squad has completed the course with no drop outs gentlemen well done.' The news that we had expected came through on the radio news today the 7th May, 1945 the Germans have surrendered, when this information was relayed to the men it was greeted with an enormous cheer. Colour Sergeant Jackson added that they were still fighting the Japanese in Burma and that the yanks were progressing slowly in the Philippines and still shipping to many American body bags home. 'So we still need to work hard as we may need to go and help out the Americans in the Far East, so no slacking lads' he said. In early June 650 and 651 squads passed out the Commando Training and only 4 men failed to make it and were back squaded. Sam's old friend now General Farquason-Keith attended the pass out parade and awarded the men there green berets so that the men could relax after 8 hectic weeks Sam issued a 48 hour pass to all of them.

In the relative quiet of the mess Colour Sergeant Jackson was centre stage in front of all his Instructors and they seemed to be enjoying themselves with lots of laughter breaking the silence. The three officers sat together which left the General and Sam sitting alongside each other at a table with a wonderful view across the river Exe. 'When the fighting in Burma and the Philippines is over I'm going to leave the Corps sir', said Sam 'I thought you were a lifer, Sam', said the General. 'When I left Burma I was pleased to leave all that blood, sweat and death behind, I'd had enough, and with the medal and all, I didn't want to become a manipulated Department of Defence puppet, going around waving the Union Jack' he said. 'Appreciate that Sam, but I'll be sorry to see you go', said the General. 'When I receive your letter of resignation please promise me that you will come and see me'. 'That is a promise sir' said Sam.

The summer drifted slowly on and 652 and 653 arrived from Lympstone. Sam gave more or less the same induction speech as before, but added that although the war in the Pacific was nearing the end, you guys need to be aware of the violent and unstable nature of countries in the Far East and made the point of stressing the finer points of jungle warfare. In a bid to end the fighting in the Philippines the Americans dropped two atom bombs on Japan, one on Hiroshima and one on Nagasaki. This was on the 9th August. That was enough for the Japanese to surrender on 15th August, 1945.

Not the best way to end a war, thought Sam, killing all those civilians, but according to the American President, *"It will stop any further bloodshed in the Far East and allow our boys back home."*

Chapter 25

He resigned from the Corps the next day by letter to the General and promised not to leave before the 6th October when 652 and 653 had completed their training. As promised, he arranged to meet with the General on the last day in September and they chatted on what Sam was to do when he left the Corps.

'One last favour Sam' said the General, 'I want you to go and see a Commander James Lansbury, he works for MI5 and he has shown a lot of interest in you over the last few years'.

'I can do that', said Sam. 'I'll call and set up an appointment for you', the General said picking up the phone. After talking to Lansbury the General said, 'Is Thursday good for you Sam?'

Sam nodded to the General and the appointment booked for 10.30 am a, MI5 Headquarters, Curzon Street, Mayfair, London W1.

When he got back to camp he telephoned Katherine and they arranged to meet on the Wednesday for a drink and maybe a show in the West End. 'Daddy has a flat near Mayfair, we can stay there', she said.

'Sounds good to me, look forward to seeing you', said Sam gently replacing the phone in its holder. Sam again took the phone to London on the Wednesday and was met at the station by Katherine who was dressed in best blues Wren's uniform. There's something about a women in a uniform, thought Sam. They had a quick coffee at the Railway station cafeteria, then picked up Katherine s little Morris Minor and drove to daddy's Mayfair flat.

'I'm frightened to touch anything', said Sam, 'You can try me, I won't break' she said with a laugh.

They showered and dressed went to the West End for dinner and then on to a show at His Majesty's theatre.

'A lovely day, thanks Katherine', 'That sounded a little distant Sam are you trying to tell me something', she said. 'I've decided to leave the Corps', he said 'That's no surprise to me Sam' said Katherine,

'I'm going to live on a boat in Santa Barbara, it's supposed to be a luxury cruiser with six births aboard, it sounds like a big-un', said Sam. 'Is that the boat that belongs to your Doctor friend' said Katherine.

'That's right, Doctor Li is his name' said Sam. 'I'm keeping my options open though, I'm seeing a guy at the MI5 office in Curzon Street in the morning, he'll probably offer me a job' said Sam.

'Lets get back to the apartment and get close Sam ', she said. They got close all right, in fact they got close three times. It was really good to see Katherine again, she was the kind of girl to lighten up any day.

Katherine left early the next morning for the Admiralty, leaving a goodbye note telling him to take care, signed it Kate with a couple of kisses and *Love You*. He arrived at the MI5 Headquarters and was told that Commander Lansbury would be with him shortly. Sam was dressed in his khaki battle dress with creases in all the right places.

'A lot of medals Sir', A young typist said, 'Right place, right time Ma'am, they hand them out like confetti these days' said Sam with a laugh. 'Not the Victoria Cross they don't Colonel', said a quiet well educated voice, 'Come into my parlour'. Said Commander Lansbury.

'Here at MI5, we make sure that if anything threatens the UK or what's left of the British Empire is taken down and destroyed weather it be terrorists, activists, gangs or anybody causing us problems', he said, 'I have special Agents who take care of business from Naval Intelligence, SAS, and Infantry guys, all top men highly trained. As yet no Royal Marines on board. The job pays well, together with a fine pension scheme and a bonus scheme', he added.

'I hear from my friend General Keith that you have decided to go to America to seek fame and fortune, I'm here trying to persuade you otherwise Colonel', he said.

'It's true, Commander I'm off to the States on December the 5th aboard the Queen Mary, I'm going to do a bit of sight seeing and taking a bit of a break, it's been 5 years since I had a proper holiday. I'm not sure about the fame, but certainly the fortune', said Sam,

'Two things really sir, I have options to be paraded around the UK like a puppet for our recruitment people, and I've seen enough slaughter, killing and maiming in the last 5 years, to last any man a lifetime' said Sam, 'So I'm both honoured and flattered to have been asked to join your elite outfit sir, but I'm sorry it's a no.

'That's a shame Colonel, but anticipated, so we can call off our surveillance team and get them off your back', said the Commander,

'I've been watched' said Sam not believing what the Commander had said. 'We have had our eye on you for two years at work and at play', said the Commander.

'You'll be telling next how many times I've made love recently' said Sam,

'Four times with Trisha Jevons and six times with Sir Keith Templeton's daughter Kate', said the Commander, 'Jesus, how many times do you think I will make love this afternoon', said Sam jokingly.

'None Colonel you have reserved a seat on the express train to Exeter Central at 3pm today, in fact you had better get on your way young man' he said.

'I guessed that you wouldn't be taking up the offer from us, so I've written a little note for you, you can collect it from one of the girls before you leave' said Commander Lansbury,

'I'm glad we met Colonel ', he said rising from his seat with an outstretched hand. 'Good luck across the pond'. Sam shook his hand and left the Commanders office and grabbed a cab to the station, he boarded the train, settled in his seat and opened the letter from Lansbury.

"*When you get to the States, Sam I want you to get in touch with General Alexander Boyd-Richards at the Pentagon, I have informed him of your arrival time in New York and I have also made available your personal file to him. Please make contact with him on your arrival in N Y and set up an appointment. Alex is Military Intelligence, somewhere between the FBI and*

the CIA. He is responsible to one man in the White House and that man has the ear to the President.
His address is:

> *American Military Intelligence*
> *Pentagon*
> *Arlington County*
> *Virginia.*

Good Luck Sam." He folded the letter and placed it in his breast pocket of his Battle Dress tunic.

He arrived at Exeter to be met by Sonny his Batman in a staff car and was ferried to Bickleigh. He went straight to his room and sat down to complete the paperwork for his MG to be transported to California, and to confirm his booking on the Queen Mary.

The next morning he dispatched a driver to Southampton to drop off the MG for transit, he then packed things in a trunk that wouldn't be needed on the trip and arranged for them to be freighted to LA. Finally he packed a separate bag with all the necessary items he required for the trip, officially he was still a Colonel in the Royal Marines until 1st January 1946, so he decided to wear his battle dress for the journey to New York. It was his final day at the Commando school and he called a meeting in the Mess of all Officers and NCO' Inductors. The new Commanding Officer Colonel Freddie Painter was also present.

'Its goodbye time' Sam began 'Colonel Paynter will be taking over tomorrow and he is a very fortunate man to be taking over here at Bickleigh said Sam.

'I was talking to Colour Sergeant Jackson earlier today about the wonderful team spirit that has been created between the Officers and the NCO Instructors. You have been a credit to me and to the Corps' he said. 'I believe you young guys call it "E'spree de Corps".

'Well, you guys have got it in abundance and as my dear friend Colour Sergeant Jackson said to me, they are as good as 'A' Troop 44 Commando, and that gentlemen, is the highest praise I can give you. I hope you continue with the new Jungle training format and with Colonel Paynter's experience in street fighting, the training package will again improve', said Sam.

So here it is, no presentations, I'm out of here with no pomp and circumstance' Sam continued. 'Now who's going to by me a beer' said Sam moving towards the bar.

Chapter 26

The next morning Sam climbed into the back of a staff car and the driver pulled away from his office for the last time, they reached the barrier and standing alone was Sergeant Len Jackson VC at attention and saluting. 'hold it for a while driver' said Sam. He got out of the car and walked over to the Colour Sergeant and returned the salute. 'It's been a pleasure and an honour serving with you Len' said Sam giving Len a bear hug. 'Back at you sir' said Len. Sam gave Len another bear hug feeling that he would probably never see his friend again. Sam eased Colours away from himself and saluted, returned to his seat in the car and instructed the driver to move out.

He arrived at Southampton Central railway station and took a taxi to the dock where the massive Queen Mary was tied up. Sam passed through the ticket office and passport control and boarded the great liner.. He located his cabin on D deck, took off his clothes and lay on the bed where he dosed for a while before falling asleep.

He woke up when a long burst on the ship's foghorn shattered his peaceful power nap. She weighed anchor and Sam was on his way to the USA.

The five day trip to New York was uneventful apart from a surprise invitation to the Captains table for dinner on the 2nd night of the voyage.

'How's your cabin Colonel' asked the Captain, 'Very comfortable thank you sir, but not to much of a view, I'm on D deck' said Sam, 'This not good a war veteran with a VC on D deck, goodness me', said the Captain, as he called over the First Officer and whispered in his ear, The Officer immediately left the table and out of the dining room.

The evening went pleasantly enough with Sam doing his officers duty by dancing with all the old rich ladies making up the Captains party. Sam returned to his seat after coping with an old dear who couldn't even dance a modern waltz and studied the dessert menu.

The Captain moved in along side Sam and said 'The key to your new cabin on A deck Colonel, your things have been moved in, I can't have VC holders sleeping in the dungeons', he said with a laugh. At midnight Sam went to his new cabin on A deck and opened the porthole and listened to the water passing along the hull of the ship, it was almost ghost like. He undressed and climbed into his bed and slept till dawn.

The big ship docked in New York five days after departing from Southampton. Sam stood on the starboard side of the giant ship leaning right up against the rail scanning the dock for a site of Jon Jo Li. He collected his bags and made his way down the gangplank.

Sam looked around and saw his friend Doc John Jo Li smiling from ear to ear. 'Colonel Sam' he said flinging his arms around Sam for what seemed an eternity. 'It's great to see you John Jo, what is it five years, and your all grown up' said Sam. Doctor Li took Sam's luggage and asked Sam to follow him to his car. 'Lets show you a bit of Manhattan, welcome to the "Big Apple" Sam' he said. They arrived at John Jo's place, and what a place it was, Fifth Avenue. John Jo parked the car in his reserved spot in the underground car park under his apartment and then took the elevator to the ground floor, then swapped lifts and the Doc pressed the button for the penthouse. When the lift door opened at the penthouse floor Sam turned to the Doc and said, '"Jesse" how the other half live'.

"This is nothing Colonel Sam, wait till you see my pad in California" he said. Sam was shown to his room which overlooked 5th Avenue and down town Manhattan. Sam had never seen anything like it, the view was sensational.

'Take a shower Colonel Sam and then we will take food at Dempsey's '. It's amazing what women will do to look younger, breast enhancement, tiny asses, nose jobs and slim figures and are willing to pay big bucks or their husband does, to try to retain their youth'.

'I have two clinics one in Santa Barbara, California and one in Manhattan, the two big money areas, I have four Surgeons working in both clinics and as they say in this part of the world, I have money to burn'.

'I have a beautiful home in Santa Barbara, a large luxury yacht at the Marina, and this apartment here on 5th Avenue. Two cars one here and one on the west coast'

'While you are here in the United States and I hope it's a long time, you have a room here and a big boat to stay on in Santa Barbara. You will not pay a red cent for any of the accommodation' and of course you have access to both sets of wheels', said the Doctor.

'You are a kind man Doctor John Li' said Sam.

'I've got a trip to make down to Virginia to see a guy at the Pentagon, it's more of a favour really for a chap in the British Secret Service. When that's taken care of, I'll get my ass off to California' said Sam.

I would like to see some of the sites in New York, while I'm here, especially the empire State Building, the Chrysler Centre, Wall Street and the Brooklyn Botanical Gardens'

'OK call me with your ETA at Los Angeles and I'll arrange for you to be picked up and transported to the boat, Probably by my little sister'. 'Spud! Is she here', said Sam. 'Shipped her over four years ago, she's at Berkeley studying photography', said the Doctor.

Chapter 27

The following morning Sam made the call to General Boyd-Richards III and arranged to see him late afternoon tomorrow in Virginia. A note slipped under Sam's door just confirmed that a vehicle was ready and waiting for him, parked in my space in the underground parking area. It was signed John Jo.

Sam packed an overnight bag, put it on the back seat of the Chevrolet and hung his battle dress tunic on a hook just above the offside rear window. He pulled out into the busy New York traffic and picked up the sign for the 1 – 95 which took him out of the city, he kept on going until he met route 66 West to Virginia, six hours later he pulled into a small motel approximately 30 miles from his destination.

He took a shower, changed and left his room, took the bridge walk way over the freeway and sat down in a burger joint and had a meal. When he finished he returned to his room stripped off, got into bed and slept soundly until 8am the next day.

He left the motel a little after 10am and drove the 30 odd miles to the Pentagon and after passing numerous road blocks he finally obtained his visitors pass. He parked the Chevy in the visitors' car park and made his way to the reception desk. He told a lady naval officer that he was a tad early for his appointment, he added that he could murder a coffee, she smiled and directed him towards the restaurant. Sam browsed through a Time magazine until it was time to report back to the reception area.

'Colonel Lassiter' a young attractive navy officer called out 'the General will see you now sir'.

'It's a bit of a trek to the Generals office sir, this place is like a small city', she said climbing in the driver's seat of what looked like a golf buggy.

'Hop on sir', she said.

Sam sat on the buggy facing backwards to the way they were travelling. He was amazed how massive the Pentagon was corridor after corridor of endless grey tiles.

'This is it sir' she said pulling up in front of door 1326, 'Get one of the girls to call me when you have finished Colonel and I'll come and collect you and return you to reception.'

'Many thanks Lieutenant' said Sam.

I'm sure they pick the staff at the Pentagon by studying "Penthouse" magazine, as all the lady naval officers were drop dead gorgeous, thought Sam.

'Straight ahead sir, the General will see you now' said another raving beauty.

A booming mid west voice rang out 'Good afternoon young man, Sam isn't it', 'Yep that's me General and a good afternoon to you to sir', said Sam.

'I've been looking at your profile young man, Commander Lansbury has kindly sent me a copy and I like what I see', the General said.

'The outfit I run here at the Pentagon is similar to that of MI5 and MI6 in the UK, maybe not so sophisticated yet, but we are getting there', he continued.

'Any individual, gang, suspected terrorist or the like that threaten the good old USA, we find them and snuff them out', he said.

'Bottom line I want you to come and work for me Sam, I'll pay you $100,000 a year, supply some wheels, an excellent pension and welfare package and an open expense account when you are on assignment.' 'What do you say young man?' 'Sounds good to me General, lets give it a go', said Sam.

'Before you commit pen to paper there are a couple of things you may not particularly like', said the General.

'Go for it General', said Sam. 'You will have to lose your name, Colonel Lassiter VC DSO George Cross RM. Rtd, most organisations are clever enough to carry out research on certain individuals and with your track record you'd be a sitting target.

'No problem I'd like to use my mothers maiden name if I may. Her name was Collins'.

'Collins it is then I'll get that sorted' said the General.

'One other thing how do you feel about becoming an American Citizen, Sam?',

'It's not a problem for me Sir, go for it', said Sam. 'Great to have you on board Agent Sam Collins, fill in a couple of forms on your way out and I'll be in touch when you forward to me your new address in California.

'Thank you Sir', said Sam and made his way to the outer office where he completed forms for the equivalent of the official secrets act, American citizenship and personal information for a name change.

He drove out of the Pentagon, returned the salute at the main gate and proceeded north to pick up route 66 and 1 – 95 to New York City.

Seven hard driving hours later he arrived in Manhattan and after passing the underground entrance to John Jo's apartment three times finally located the correct turn off, and parked in Dr. Li's space. He took the lift to the reception area, gave Spencer a wave and made his way across to the elevator to the penthouse. He let himself in to the suite and sat down on his bed, he then stripped off his clothes and put on a white towel dressing gown that the Doc had left him. All his washing and ironing had been done while he was away and Sam thought this guy thinks of everything.

On the dressing table was an envelope with Sam's name on it, he opened it to find an air ticket, club class one way only from La Guardia to Los Angeles. The flight time was 10.30am tomorrow, a little note attached to the ticket said that '*I'll send someone along to meet you in L.A.*' Signed John Jo.

The following morning, Sam finished his packing and then started on the four 'S's', shave, shower, shampoo, the 4th s was his daily ritual. He buzzed Simpson at the front desk and got him to order a taxi and made his way down to the reception area. 'Your cab is here' said Simpson, 'I'll be seeing you again Simmo', said Sam leaving the building.

A dirty yellow cab was idling on the forecourt.' 'Where do you wanna go', said the driver, Sam replied in a voice that reminded him of Lance Templeton, 'La Guardia Airport please young man' said Sam

When they arrived at the Departure gate at the terminal the driver said 'That'll be 10 bucks' Sam gave him twenty dollars and said,'The extra 10 is not a tip, it's for you to clean this heap, the inside is like a public shit house'. Sam got his bag out of the taxi himself and went directly to the Western Airlines counter and stood in line.

He boarded the aircraft and was directed to a window seat on row H, a few moments later a tall elegant looking girl was struggling to put her carry on in the overhead locker. Sam eased out of his seat and said 'I'll get that' and shoved her bag in the overhead. 'I'm Samantha' she said,' 'We have a problem then Ma'am' said Sam 'I'm a Sam too'. She gave a nervous laugh and sat down in her seat her long legs just about managing to fit in to the space provided. The aircraft was pushed out from the loading bay and slowly made it's way to the take off runway. The pilot aligned the aircraft ready for take off, Sam looked at his new travelling companion and saw that she was visibly shaking and white knuckling both seat arms.

'It's my first time on a plane and I'm petrified' she said. Change the subject and keep her talking thought Sam.

'What do you do for a living then Samantha' said Sam, 'I'm a model' she said, 'It's got to be stockings or short dresses with those long legs of yours' said Sam 'Actually it's lingerie, I'm off to my first shoot in Los Angeles' she said.

Sam gave her some chewing gum telling her that she should always chew something when the aircraft was taking off, it stops yours ears popping on our way up to cruising altitude. 'Another thing to remember is that it is more dangerous crossing the street than it is to fly' he said.

'I'm from Wisconsin' she said we sometimes get two cars a day down Main Street'. They both laughed at this and Sam could see that she had settled down a little. 'What's going to happen now is' said Sam as the plane lined itself up for take off, 'The engines will roar and we will be on our way, there is nothing to worry about' said Sam placing his hand gently on top of hers on the arm rests.

The aircraft achieved take off speed and soured into the sky leaving a cloudy New York behind them. When they reached the cruising altitude Sam removed his hand and said 'You did good Samantha'. The flight to Chicago was uneventful with Samantha still clinging on to the arms of her seat.

The view coming into Chicago was fantastic, with all the huge skyscrapers clustered together on the edge of lake Michigan. After we landed an announcement by the Pilot that we would be on the ground for one hour and that drinks and cold food would be made available.

Samantha went to the toilet to fresh up a little and on her return to her seat looked so much more relaxed. The paleface gone, a hint of perfume and make up professionally applied, she looked a doll thought Sam.

'What about you then Sam, what are you going to do now that the fighting is over'

'I'm going to chill a bit and catch up with old friends, maybe do a bit of security work', he lied.

'I was in the Royal Marines 44 Commando stationed in Burma fighting the Japanese for 5 years.

'You must be good at your job looking at all your medals' said Samantha', 'Just the same as everybody else' said Sam.

The plane took off again bound for Portland, Oregon on the west coast. Somebody turned the heating up and most of the passengers dosed off. They touched down at Portland and Sam woke up to find Samantha's head resting on his shoulder. 'Oh I'm sorry Sam' said Samantha sitting bolt upright in her seat, 'Where are we?' 'Portland on the west coast, we'll be here for an hour'.

After an hour they were on their way again hugging the west coast, flying over San Francisco and well on their way to the final destination. 'I'd really like to know how your first shoot went Samantha' said Sam'. "I'm staying at the Holiday Inn in Burbank' she said handing Sam a hotel flyer.

They touched down right on schedule, taxied to the terminal and into the baggage claim. Sam stood alongside Samantha at the luggage carousel and when her bags arrived removed them for her.

'Goodbye and good luck Sam' she said, 'Back at you' replied Sam.

Sam left the baggage claim and entered crowded arrival area, and spotted a very attractive young lady holding up a sign that read Lassiter.

Sam made his way over to the girl and said 'Hi I'm Sam Lassiter'. 'Yes I know you are Colonel Sam' she said. 'You don't recognise me do you' she said. Sam took a closer look at the pretty girl and said 'Spud is that you?'. 'You are the only man in the world allowed to call me that, Colonel Sam."

They both walked to the set down area and climbed into a brightly coloured jeep, 'Put your bag on the back seat and let's roll' she said.

They slipped out of the airport and headed north on the coast road for the 85 mile trip to Santa Barbara,

She took the 2nd turn off for Santa Barbara and headed for the marina. On arrival she stopped at a gate, entered a code, the gate opened and she drove through. She drove passed some lovely looking boats before stopping opposite a 175 foot luxury cruiser.

'So where is my little fishing boat that is to be my home for the next few months' he said looking at a nice little compact fishing boat to the right of the cruiser.'

'You can use the little boat if you want but this is your new home Colonel Sam' she said pointing to the luxury cruiser.

'It's beautiful' said Sam following the girl up the gangplank and on the craft

'My brother got her cheap as the guy who bought her couldn't keep up with the payments, apparently according to my brothers lawyer, it's a good tax dodge'.

'I don't think John has ever been aboard her so it's good that you can stay and live on board' said Monique.

'I'll show you around properly tomorrow, after I have taken you shopping; you look terribly European and square' she said.

'OK "spud" I'll see you in the morning' said Sam. 'Unless you want me to spend the night here on board' she said.

'10.30 in the morning, goodbye, OK "Spud"' said Sam

She nodded a farewell OK, planted a kiss on Sam's cheek and left, 'Later' she said. Sam sat down and relaxed in one of the luxurious lounge sofas and fell asleep, he was absolutely knackered after a frantic few days.

He got up at 7am and wrote a note to General Richards at the Pentagon informing him of his new address and phone number. Monique turned up smack on 10.30 and they both set off to buy Sam a new wardrobe. They returned at 3pm and Sam dumped his new buys in the cabin he had selected to sleep in, then they both walked across the docks to Filippo's for lunch. Monique had some bits and bobs to get together for her final week at Berkeley so with another peck on Sam's cheek she left.

'Have a nice weekend Sam'

'You too "Spud" said Sam.

Sam had a quiet peaceful weekend and was well rested by the time he started writing overdue letters to Katherine, Len and Lady Templeton. The old General was not a 5 day week person, as Sam picked up a note that lay on the floor outside the cabin door. The note said that a registered letter awaited to be collected from the U.S. Postal which was situated directly opposite the "John Jo"

He collected the letter and informed the guy behind the counter that future letters could be addressed to Colonel Lassiter or Sam Collins which he said was his pen name.

'No problem sir!' the clerk replied.

The next few days were routine, a morning 3-mile run, lunch at Filippo's and letter writing in the afternoons whilst sitting out in the sunshine on the flying bridge dressed in a tee shirt, shorts, sunglasses, baseball cap and new running shoes. He was just about to leave when he spotted a stray piece of paper sticking out of his wallet, he looked at it, frowned and thought why on earth would I write down a phone number and put my own name by the side of it.

'Shit it's Samantha the model he met on the plane on his flight from New York. He picked up the phone and dialed the number

'Holiday Inn, can I help you?' 'I need to talk Samantha somebody. I don't know her surname but her address when she registered would be somewhere in Wisconsin' said Sam' 'Hold on I'll see what I can do' said the receptionist, 'Here we go putting you through sir' she said. A sleepy voice answered 'Samantha speaking 'Who's calling in the middle of the night', 'It's the other Sam here the guy you met on the plane'

'Oh Sam it's great to hear from you, how are you settling in on the boat?' she said.

'I'm good, how did the shoot go?' said Sam, 'Really well, they really looked after me and were very professional. They paid me a chunk of money and promised me more work when they introduce there new summer fashions, 'Great, I'm so pleased for you' said Sam.

'I do have a problem though Sam, I was introduced to a guy from Dolphin swimwear who said that he was very impressed with the lingerie shoot and asked me for a copy of my Swimwear portfolio. The problem is I haven't got one'

'The fashion photographer's out here in California cost an absolute fortune so I think I will pass on the Dolphin thing' said Samantha.

'I have an idea, my friend out here has a sister who has just successfully completed her finals at Berkeley in Film and Photography, what if I give her a call and set something up' said Sam. She is called Monique and will soon be opening her new studio in Santa Barbara, 'That would be magic' she said.

'OK, be here in the morning around 10.30 and I'll arrange for Monique to be here. She can grab some Dolphin swimsuits and a bunch of bikinis.' he said. Before he put down the phone he left the name of the boat and the address of the marina. He also had an after thought and gave her the password to open the marina gate.

He phoned John Jo's place and asked to talk to Monique, only to be told that she was working getting her new studio up and running. He was given the address by Manuel.

Sam ran out of the marina, through a park and on to the road leading to down town Santa Barbara. Sam could see why Santa Barbara was called the American Riviera, he passed some beautiful Sevilla luxury residences close to the beach which were so sophisticated but casual. A guy was erecting a modern style sign which said *Studio Monique* and another two men finishing off the outside painting in pink, white and a hint of light grey. Sam went inside and saw Monique covered in sawdust talking earnestly to the carpenter.

'Hello Colonel Sam welcome to Studio Monique', 'Very impressive' said Sam. 'I've got an idea and I'd like to run it across you' said Sam. 'I think I have landed your first commission', said Sam,

'You have got to stop kidding me Colonel Sam my studio is serious business'.

'The girl I met on the plane, Samantha is her name has just completed a successful lingerie shoot for Vogue International and she would like to meet you and put together a Swimwear portfolio. 'We meet at the boat tomorrow. What do you say?' said Sam.

'I don't know what to say Sam', 'Just say yes and be there at 10.30 in the morning' he said jogging off back to the marina.

The following morning Samantha let herself in to the marina and drove slowly around until she found the John Jo and parked her car next to Sam's MG that was recently taken out of a holding warehouse. She got out of her Chevy and looked around.

'Hi Samantha' Sam called from the nearby Filippo's nursing a coffee,'Hello Sam it's really nice of you to try and help me' said Samantha, 'Not a problem' said Sam.

They were both chatting away, Sam about his luxury cruiser and Samantha about her recent lingerie shoot, when Monique came rocketing around the corner in her little jeep. She screeched to a halt and was out of the vehicle before the engine died. 'Morning "Spud", 'Morning to both of you, mine's a latte please and a bagel' said Monique, The two girls hit it off straight away.

Chapter 28

'I can't thank you enough for helping me out with this, it could turn out to be very important' said Samantha. 'I will make you more beautiful than you already are, so let's get busy' said Monique.

'I'll leave you guys to it, if there is any heavy lifting to do Monique, gimme a call' said Sam. Who then returned to his cabin to finish off some letters to friends back home in the UK.

Two hours later the girls were still at it Monique directing things and Samantha responding. All the shots so far had been on board the John Jo or on the quay side ensuring that only million dollar cruisers were in the back drop.

'OK, I'm good here, Sam can you help me get the gear up to Malibu so that we can get some beach shots. When we've finished there we can take the final shots at my place by the pool' she said.

'OK that's it. I'm happy and Samantha you were wonderful' she said.

'It's going to take me a few days to pick out the best photo's and to have a chat with my graphic designer to complete a professional presentation, we'll talk about money if your man likes what he see's, I'll be in touch in a few days Samantha' said Monique.

Two days passed and Monique phoned Sam and said 'It's the best work I've ever done Sam I hope she likes it'. 'She'll love it, come on over to the boat and I'll phone Samantha and get her along.

Monique and Samantha arrived at the boat at more or less the same time and greeted each other with a huge hug and sat down at Filippo's and ordered some coffees.

'And who is this young man you have brought with you Samantha' looking at the guy straight between the eyes.

'Let me introduce myself Sam, I'm David Bergson President of Dolphin Sports and Swimwear' said the man leaning across the table with arm outstretched.

'Pleased to meet you David' said Sam. 'And you must be the super designer Monique, I'm looking forward to seeing your work I've heard some good things about you young lady, so I thought I'd come along and meet you face to face if that's OK?' he said.

'If it's OK with "Spud" then it's OK with me', said Sam.

'I'm "Spud by the way Mr. Bergson, it's very nice to meet you' said Monique.

The moment of truth, thought Monique, as she reached into her holdall and removed a white bag that had a Studio Monique logo on it, from the inside she pulled out a beautifully bound white leather folder with gold trim entitled Swimwear, and below the title Samantha Raven.' Along the bottom printed in smaller gold letters Studio Monique, Santa Barbara, California.

Monique handed the file over to Samantha.

She opened it up with David looking over her shoulder.

'Wonderful' said Samantha.

'Superb job Monique, the photo's are stunning, I'm prepared to offer you a contract with Dolphin for you to continue to carry out photo shoots for the whole of the Dolphin Group of companies. Monique gave a yelp sprung to her feet and gave David a huge hug. 'Thank so much I'm so happy' said Monique. 'Congratulations to you too Miss Raven you look sensational in these pictures', David said.

'Lets set up a meeting say next Saturday at Studio Monique to dot the eyes and cross the tee's', said David.

'Very good I'll set it up' said Monique.

The party then padded down the wooden jetty across the concrete quayside towards Filippo's restaurant, they could hear Filippo's powerful tenor voice coming from the kitchen area. Filippo was a huge fan of Mario Lanza and would often burst into song as he served his customers.

The four of them ate lunch, after which David and Samantha departed.

'See you on Saturday morning Monique'. Said David pulling away in his car with Samantha.

'We did it Colonel Sam', said Monique.

'We didn't do anything "Spud" you did it all, well done, good job', said Sam.

'Take John or one of his lawyers to the meet on Saturday, you need a legal guy to go over things before putting pen to paper.' Sam continued.

'I'll talk to my brother and get it sorted', she said, 'One more thing, I want you there as well Colonel Sam'. She left the marina in her little jeep and waved Sam goodbye.

Sam was relaxing in the lounge area of the boat when he heard a familiar voice.

'Mail call for Mr. Sam Collins', 'Hi Marlon I'll take that', said Sam.

Sam signed on receipt of the registered letter, that was post marked West Virginia. He waited until the mail man had left the boat and opened the letter. The letter read:

Hi Sam, I trust you are settled in OK. I have your first assignment, I have enclosed the most accurate surveillance data we have.

Basically a Cuban run drug cartel is trying to widen it's market and is targeting New York, the most recent drug dropped on the Bronx area was a bad one and several young druggies have died.

It will take me a week to organize things in New York. You will be going to the 52nd precinct in the Bronx as a London Met' Policeman seeing how things are done this side of the water. You will be working with Sergeant Stacey and Detective Bonetti. I want you to crush this cartel before it's really up and running.

Let's look at Monday week for you to be in New York. Regards Alex.

He would take a long look at the intel provided in the additional enclosed envelope later today after he had finished off the letters to Len and Lady Janet Templeton. As Sam opened the door to let in some fresh air he noticed a flyer on the deck just outside the lounge. The flyer was advertising an art auction sale at Sotherby's New York in two weeks time, the paintings up for auction included some great American painters. He added a P.S. to Lady Janet's letter informing her of the auction and asked her for guidance on if she wanted to participate. He listed the names of the artists whose work was up for auction. He completed the two letters and shoved them into the U.S. Postal box.

Sam returned to the boat and spoke to John Jo and Monique and informed them that he had to go to New York and swat a few flies away, he would be flying off next Monday so he will be able to attend the meeting with David Bergman on Saturday.

'You must stay in the penthouse in New York'. John Jo said to Sam.

The meeting at Studio Monique went well with Stu Maxwell giving Monique the nod to sign the contract document. Before Sam left he was pulled aside by Monique and she said.

'I've talked to my brother and we both agree that you should be a part of Studio Monique, we propose that you will be a 10% shareholder in the company, John will take a 30% share and I will take the majority 60%.

'You mean I'm a sleeping partner' said Sam, 'I hope so, especially the sleeping bit', said Monique.

'Behave yourself "Spud" said Sam.

'Can you take me to the Airport on Monday morning, say 8am at the boat, we can take the MG and you can use it while I am away', said Sam.

'OK see you and 8am on Monday' said Monique ending the call.

Sam finished packing, left a note at the U.S. Postal with his address in New York in case any mail needed to be re-directed. The last job before departing for New York was to make a cheque out for Monique Li for $20,000, he placed it in an envelope and left it on the lounge table. Monique drove the MG to the Airport and didn't say too much, finally she said as they entered the departure area,

'I don't want you to go, every time you left on a patrol in Burma I didn't want you to go!' she said.

'Don't worry "Spud" It won't take to long to brush a few flies away.' he said.

She dropped him off at the set-down area just outside the departures. Sam said his goodbyes, Monique said nothing, waved and roared off in the little sports car.

Chapter 29

Sam boarded the plane and slid into his window seat, turned on the overhead reading light, opened the envelope and studies the information supplied by the General on the Cuban drug cartel. He particularly had a good look at the profiles of the prominent players. He fell asleep and didn't wake until the decent on O Hare Airport, Chicago. A stewardess stopped at his seat and passed him some photo's that had fallen in the aisle when he fell asleep.

'They looked important, so I placed them back inside the envelope' she said,

'Sorry to be so clumsy Ma'am and yes they are important, thank you so much'. What a bloody idiot thought Sam, a fine secret agent me.

The Strato cruiser landed safely at New York La Guardia Airport and then Sam took a cab to Manhattan and the penthouse on Fifth Avenue. He was really tired out and after a shower, stripped off his clothes and went to bed. He slept soundly until 6am the following morning, he dressed in casual trousers a navy blue shirt and his favourite pilots brown fur lined jacket.

Sam didn't want to come across as a complete idiot so he did a bit of ground work on the Bronx before he met the two Detectives. The Bronx was the most northerly of the 5 boroughs of New York City covering 42 square miles including the famous Zoo and the equally famous Yankee Stadium. He also noted that there was a lot of poverty and poor properties in the area. A surprise was that the Bronx was the greenest of the 5 Boroughs. Sam thought London was busy but New York was like nothing he had ever seen before, thousands of people packing the sidewalk, 20 deep, all with their heads down and hurrying to there place of work.

He took the Metro down town, then changed lines and travelled on to the Bronx. Before he left the apartment he had called the Duty Desk Sergeant who supplied him with the directions to get to the 52nd precinct. He stood outside the building and cast an eye over it, dirty 4 story grey stone building. A car park that was to small to cater for the number of squad cars jockeying for a parking spot. He entered the precinct, the place brightly lit, very noisy and full of Cops, would be thugs and hookers. The Desk Sergeant was barking out orders over a microphone, with nobody taking to much interest, drug addicts were throwing up on the floor and the hookers were sitting on the benches with there legs wide apart, some had knickers on and some didn't.

'Can I help you young fella?' a hoarse voice bellowed from behind a tall desk.

'I'm here to meet Sergeant Stacey and Detective Bonetti, I'm the Copper' on loan from the UK' said Sam.

'Go straight through that door and get out of this shit storm!' he said.

Sam was just about to enter the door when he heard a guy yell; 'Who dares?, who fuckin' dares?' he was standing with a flick knife in his hand just having slashed a women police officer who was now bleeding from the shoulder.

'No guns, too many people in the house' yelled the desk Sergeant

'Who dares?' the young thug said again. 'I dare' said Sam walking straight up to face the guy. The guy made two slashes in thin air, then started waving the knife around,

'Are you sure you want to do this, it's going to be a painful end for you' said Sam.

'Fuck off' pig!' he said with another slash of the blade. As the blade flashed towards Sam he parried the thrust and at the same time drilled his boot hard into the guys balls, the guy doubled over, Sam straightened him up with a knee to the jaw and finally delivered a punch just under the bridge of the guys nose, which laid him out cold.

'Jesus that was fast "Limey"', said the desk Sergeant.

'Not really did you see his eyes, they were shot, gone, lost, nobody at home, drugged up, so I gave him a bit of a slap', said Sam.

'Get an ambulance for the lady Sarge but don't worry to much about this heap of shit on the floor.' The whole 'act of aggression' took less than 20 seconds

'Is this the correct door Sarge?' he said wandering slowly across the blood soaked floor.

Sam entered the detectives room where a dozen or so detectives were chatting to each other about Sam's antics in the main reception area, while the others were drinking coffee from an automatic dispenser.

Sam walked up to an enormous black guy and said, 'I'm looking for Sergeant Stacey and Detective Bonetti'

'They're with the Lieutenant she shouldn't be to long, take a seat, that's her desk' he said pointing to a desk in the corner of the room. 'I'm Fred Palmer by the way', 'Sam Collins' said Sam,

'Do they teach the British cops that kind of combat' said Detective Palmer"

'No I just learned a trick or two in the Marines' said Sam. 'Good to meet you Sam' said Palmer.

Five minutes later a striking blonde and a tubby middle aged women emerged from the Lieutenants office. Sam stood up as the blonde slid into her seat and Bonetti in hers opposite.

'Shit that guy has some mouth on him' referring to Lieutenant Briggs.

Turning slightly to the left and looking directly at Sam, she said 'So, you are the cop from the UK who is going to show us how to run a police squad?'

'I was under the impression that you and Detective Bonetti were going to show me the ropes' said Sam.

'Ah we have a smart ass' said Stacey.

'If I was a smart ass I'd be working out of the Chief of Police offices in Albany not this shit house' said Sam.

'Point taken, I'm Sergeant Christine Stacey and this lady is my partner Detective Mary Jo Bonetti' she said reaching across the desk and offering a hand to Sam,

'Nice to meet you folks, who wants coffee?' said Sam walking over to the vending machine

'Not that rubbish, lets go over to Grazianno's, the Sarge is paying', said Mary Jo.

Guiding Mary Jo out of the building he said 'Where's the cafe?',

'Lets go over the crossing, it's right there, see,' said Mary Jo pointing across the street.

A large black women greeted them as they entered and said 'What can I get yah?'

'Two latte's and a regular coffee', said Mary Jo.

'Anything to eat, the lady asked'

'Not for us we're dieting, Sam anything for you?' said Chris,

'I'll take an egg "sarnie" please, egg sunny side up', said Sam,

'Jesus we have found a gentleman in the middle of the Bronx', said the big lady behind the counter.

The three of them sat down and formerly introduced themselves. Chris said she was single, but engaged to be married to a Senator who seems to be two timing her according to the daily gossip column in the newspaper. She said she was following in her dad's footsteps, as he was a veteran cop until he got gunned down by a druggie. Mary Jo was married to a guy called Henry and had two kids a boy and a girl and she lived out of town in New Jersey. Sam told them he was an ex Marine and had only been with the Met' a year and that's one of the reasons he is here to learn.

'Two latte's, one regular and one egg sandwich with the egg looking at yah', said the big lady.

All went quiet as they all gazed out of the dirty window watching the hoards of people scurrying along the pavement, none of them looking particularly happy with there lot.

'Tough town' said Sam,

'There are some nice parts of New York city Sam, I'll show you around when we have a little more time' said Chris Stacey,

'I'd like that' he said.

'I hear you caused a bit of a ruckus in the precinct this morning Sam, what was that all about?' asked Mary Jo,

'A kid cut a police officer, so I took the knife off him and knocked him out, it was no big deal really, the guy was on drugs, shaking like a leaf and he wasn't holding the knife right, I think he had been watching to many Cop movies' said Sam. 'Do you think we could go and see the lady cop who was injured?', said Sam.

'I'll arrange it Sam, I believe she's at the Lincoln Hospital here in the Bronx'. said Mary Jo.

They finished their coffee and left the cafe waited at the crossing for the green man to appear and then walked directly to the police car park to pick up there ride, 'I'll just go and pick up a few things from my desk, I won't be long' said Chris, 'Do you want to come with me Sam?' she said,

'I think it would be a good idea to leave me in the car park, there's probably a bit of a "Hoo Hah" going on in there at the moment', said Sam, pointing to the entrance of the 52nd precinct.

Within 5 minutes they were cruising the streets of New York. At the risk of repeating himself, Sam told them that he had fought in Burma with the Royal Marines in World Two and on leaving joined the Metropolitan Police in London, England. I've been recruited to try and formulate a more accurate and detailed profiling program' said Sam. I'm interested to see if a more accurate profiling can assist the Cop' on the beat', he said.

'The kind of intel' we get at the moment ain't too hot' said Chris. She continued by saying 'It's more seat of your pants stuff, we don't rely too much on profiling Sam' she said.

'Same with me Sam it just doesn't do it for me' said Mary Jo.

'While I'm in the States I shall be hooking up with the FBI, CIA, NYPD and LAPD profiler's with a brief to get faster and more accurate profile information out there, especially in major crimes' said Sam.

Mary Jo and Chris Stacey filled in more of their situations both at work with NYPD and their private status. 'You know most things about me Sam, I'm the daughter of a cop as I said before. My dad was shot in the face by some drugged up kid and at present I'm engaged to recently elected Senator for New York Robert F. Mitchell, this however, may be short lived if TV pictures of him on the news shows him cuddling up to a twenty something skinny woman.

The radio crackled into life, disturbance at Whittaker Heights, number 3244 man and woman, a lot of shouting and reports from a neighbour of the women being slapped around.

'Car 42 Lacey and Bonetti responding', 'Roger to that car 42' said the operator.

Mary Jo placed the red light on the top of the car, Chris set the siren off and shoved her foot hard down on the accelerator pedal. They reached Whittaker and ran up the stairs to apartment 3244, outside the apartment sat a little girl all tucked up, knees pressed against her chest, and the mother of all rows going on inside.

'Are you armed Sam?' said Chris, 'Yep' said Sam reaching to the small of his back and producing a 9mm Beretta, 'Mary Jo look after the kid, Sam you're with me' said Chris

'Open up, this is NYPD', said Chris

'Go and fuck yourself pig' came the reply,

Sam touched Chris on the shoulder and put his finger to his lips.

'You either open up the door or we come through it, your call' said Sam.

The door slowly opened, a guy in a dirty sweat soaked singlet and holding a knife with a 6 inch double edged blade. He said 'Who told you to come here and interfere in what is family business?'

'Some business' said Sam, looking at the battered face of the woman sitting on the floor her back against the fridge crying her eyes out.

'I'll tell you what' said Sam, 'I'll give you 5 seconds to drop the knife, if you don't manage that I'll take it off you and stuff it up your ass' said Sam. 'So ask yourself, you bloody idiot, do you want a really sore ass or a ride in a nice comfortable set of wheels down town?' Sam finished.

The guy looked completely out of it when his arms went to his sides and he dropped the knife on the floor. Sergeant Stacey cuffed him and read him his rights and hustled him into the waiting police vehicle. The little girl was re-united with her Mother and they huddled together on the kitchen floor.

'Are you going to be OK honey?' said Mary Jo to the Mother.

'I've had worse than this, but this time he is out of here.' she said.

Chris went on the car radio and reported that the situation at Whittaker was resolved and that they were bringing in the prisoner now.

'Roger to that 42, good work', said the operator.

They arrived at the 52nd, Chris booked the guy in and he was locked up.'

'You write up the report Mary Jo and I'll get the coffee' said Chris,

'It's a good job I'm educated and can write good English' said Mary Jo.

'Use the "kiss" method for your report Mary Jo' said Sam' 'Kiss method, what's that?'.

'Keep it short Sherlock' Sam said laughing.

Within the hour they were back on the road, when the radio crackled on again 'Message for Detective Bonetti' said the operator.

'Go ahead' said Mary Jo.

'A Manuel Rodriges has been admitted to Lincoln Hospital and he is asking for you Mary Jo, he's been shot.

'Message received many thanks' said Mary Jo.

'Who is Manuel' said Sam.

'He's my snitch' said Mary Jo. 'Take me straight to Lincoln Hospital. Chris it could be important, you can call in on Jennie Marshall the cop that got knifed this morning?'. They arrived at the Lincoln and went their separate ways, Sam to see Jennie and Mary Jo to see Manuel. Sam was pleased to see Jennie sitting up in bed and talking to the other three girls in the room. 'Here's my hero ladies' she said, and thanked Sam for nailing the guy in the precinct.

'When you get out of here I show you how to get a knife off somebody without getting hurt' said Sam.

They had a few more things to say when Sam said that he should get back to his partners, he went over to Jennie and planted a kiss on her cheek and left the ward. Sam reached the two NYPD Officers who were standing alongside the vehicle deep in concentration, Mary Jo seemed to be upset as she wandered back and forth away from Chris Stacey.

'What's the problem Mary Jo?', said Sam.

'Manuel didn't make it, he kept saying Cubans, drugs, warehouse behind Cafe Pacifica, Cubans, Cubans' said Mary Jo.

'We arranged to meet tonight', she said.

'Lets get out of here' said Chris and got in the driver's side of the Crown Victoria.

The next few days nothing major happened at the 52nd, a few break ins and a few family squabbles, which were easily sorted. The following morning the Captain of the precinct called a meeting for all detectives.

'Morning folks and a belated welcome to Detective Sam Collins from the UK, we have two major crimes that require maximum focus. This is, of course, as well as your normal day to day duties', he continued, 'A new drug has hit town, the first batch landed on the street two days ago, it was a bad batch and three young people have died with several more very sick.' 'We are led to believe by our FBI friends that the people responsible are Cubans out of Miami trying to improve their circulation.' 'The "Fee bees" have issued some photo's of Cubans they want to interview, so all of you get your snitches busy, all info directly to me' he said.

'The second and more alarming is that a couple of retards are going around shooting people, the majority in the Washington DC area, however yesterday a young man was shot in our backyard and the bullet matches the ones taken at the seven kills already made by the perps', The profile information from the FBI is not particularly good, but you can all take a look if you want. They believe it's two white males, one mid thirties and one younger probably a relation, the weapon is a Springfield 30 caliber. The mode of transportation they again believe is a white pick-up van, that's it good hunting'. he said and returned to his office.

Sam looked at Chris and Mary Jo and said 'I see the FBI profiler's have done it again, supplying worthless rubbish, the sooner they send some of their guys over to MI5 or Interpol the better'.

'Sam, Chris, a word, this Cuban connection do you think we should follow up on what Manuel said'

'Mary Jo, yes I do but if they have taken out Manuel they probably know about you and you sweetie ain't going anywhere near the Cafe Pacifico', said Sam. They dropped off Mary Jo at the Metro and Chris drove Sam towards the penthouse on 5th.

'Do you like Italian food Chris?', said Sam,

'Love it, why?'

'You and me, it's not a date, but how about Luigi's in the village tomorrow night, we can take a wee peep at the Pacifico from there and see if we can spot any Cubans', he said.

'You've got a no date, 8pm at Luigi's, you book it' said Chris.

Chris dropped Sam off at 5th Avenue and waved a goodnight.

Sam relaxed in one of deep soft sofas and opened up his re-directed mail. Sam opened an envelope marked private and confidential and found a copy of a wire inside sent from Lady Janet Templeton, it read:

Dear Sam,

I'm coming to New York on 15th December on flight number BA 204 arriving at Idlewild at 6pm.

I will be staying in New York for 5 days, If you could meet me at the Airport that would be nice.
     That's the BOAC building.

Regards Janet.

Sam was pleased she was coming over as he wasn't to happy with having to bid with her money and of course it would be great to see the beautiful lady again. He wrote to Sotherby's and arranged for two tickets for the 17th and 18th.

He then sent a wire to his mentor General Richards at the Pentagon requesting a copy of the FBI file on the Cuban cartel and whatever the FBI had on the guy that's going around shooting people in DC and New York. He finally finished writing to Monique congratulating her on the rapid progress of her business.

He went to bed at 11pm thinking that some progress was needed on the Cuban drug business, after all, that was why he was sent to New York.

The next morning Mary Jo called Sam over to the coffee vending machine and said very quietly that 'Could you take it easy on Chris this morning as the Senator has been at it again with another woman',

'Like most politician's he can't be trusted, she should get shot of him' Sam said.

The three of them were huddled around Chris Stacey's desk sorting out the day's schedule.

'I'd like to follow up on the info that Mary Jo's snitch gave us regarding the Cuban's'. said Sam,

'So would I", echoed Mary Jo.

'OK you two go down to the village and take a coffee at Luigi's, you'll have a great view of the cafe Pacifico from there, I'll stay here and finish off yesterdays report', Said Chris.

Sam and Mary Jo took the pool car out of the car park and into the crowded three laner to Manhattan. Took a left and headed for the village. They parked up and went into Luigi's sat down in a window seat and ordered coffee. They had a perfect view of the front and right side of the Pacifico.

They observed a few smooth looking characters going in and out of the cafe, passing by two men stationed just outside the front entrance.

'Everything points to these guys being either Latino's or Cubans, my bet is Cubans' said Sam, 'Flash shiny suits, tasteless fancy shirts, fake Italian shoes and greasy hair slicked back' he said.

A Limo pulled up outside the cafe and out stepped a little rat faced guy who was immediately surrounded by three bodyguards and ferried into the cafe. 'There's our man, Rolando Carivas', said Sam.

A white pick-up van stopped opposite one of the guards, leaning out of the window engaged the guy in conversation. After much waving of hands the pick-up disappeared around the back of the cafe.

'I'd like to know what's in that truck', said Sam,
'You and me both hun', said Mary Jo.

They both ordered another coffee and a bagel and continued to watch the comings and goings for the next hour.

Luigi came over to the two cops and said 'Is everything OK?'.

'Everything is just fine' said Mary Jo.

'One thing that has always puzzled me is with all these beautiful dishes you serve up here, how do you manage to keep it so fresh, and the cafe Pacifico has also the same problem I suppose' said Sam.

'I have four huge freezers outback, they cost me many dollars but worth every red cent, as far as I know the Pacifico is not so good at storing food, but they do have a large facility round the back of their premises' Said Luigi. 'I also find it strange that they have a man patrolling outside of the warehouse' he said.

'Very strange' said Sam. 'I would like to reserve a table for two for tonight preferably this one', said Sam.

'No problem, your name sir' said Luigi', 'It's Sam, Sam Collins and 8.30 looks good.'

Mary, Jo and Sam sat quietly in the car with the engine running.

'Just drive slowly passed the rear of the building so that I can have a quick "butchers" said Sam.

'Butchers', said Mary Jo with a strange look at Sam 'Butchers Hook, means look in London slang' he said.

They passed the rear of the cafe and noticed that the pick-up was parked alongside the Limo right in front of them. 'Stop at Luigi's, I want a word with him' said Sam.

They returned to the Bronx and sat down at Chris's desk.

'I've finished yesterdays report, do you want to read it Mary Jo?, you too Sam?' said Chris.

'Nice job Sarge', said Sam.

'It's time for lunch you guys, I'm paying', Chris said, 'Sam turned towards Chris and said,

'I'll let you pay for lunch if you let me take you to dinner tonight at Luigi's, it's not a date, it's work. I've reserved a table for two for 8.30, we've got a table seat where we can observe the Pacifico all night if we want', said Sam.

'I'd love to have a not a date dinner with you Sam' said Chris Stacey.

'I'll be waiting outside your place at 8.15, make sure you bring a decent size handbag with you it's important.' Sam added.

Sam arrived outside Chris Stacey's apartment smack on 8.15, she was ready, looking very attractive and carrying a heavy looking duffle bag. She hopped in the cab smelling like she had raided the Christian Dior perfume shop. 'Luigi's please, driver, in the village', said Sam.

The cabby set them down at Luigi's, collected the fare and sped off up town towards mid Manhattan 44. They were greeted at the door by the man himself and he gave them both a hug. 'Bonjouno Sam, and your lady bonjourno bella', said Luigi.

'Hi Luigi this is my friend Chris from the office. They were directed to a window table with the same view as before, a perfect view of the Pacifico. Luigi handed out the menus and asked if they wanted any drinks.

'A bottle of your best Chianti would be nice, is that OK with you Chris?', said Sam.'

'Perfect', said Chris.

After 10 minutes, a waiter arrived at the table and enquired if they were ready to order.

'I'll take the whitebait for a starter and the spaghetti bolognese for my main' said Chris',

'And I'll take the pate and the lasagne, thanks', said Sam.

'I see you bought a nice sized duffle bag with you, can you please put these items in it' said Sam transferring items from items from his rucksack into the duffle. Passing the 3 high explosive grenades 3 spare clips of 9mm ammo and a silencer for the Beretta, which was designed and made by his friend Colour Sergeant Jackson. He then produced a strip of aluminum about a foot long and a half an inch wide which was tucked in his sock.

'What's the strip for?', said Chris,

'An old car thief taught me how to get into locked cars', he said, winking, 'The grenades were shipped in by the General via a Courier just before 4pm today.'

'I've got a call to make. I'll be exactly seven minutes, enjoy your whitebait', said Sam, who then disappeared past the counter, through the kitchen and out the back door of Luigi's place.

He stopped and fished out the grenades and armed them with 3 second fuses, he attached a piece of string three feet long to each ring. He then screwed the silencer in place on the Beretta, and approached the loan guard in front of the locked rear door.

He was four feet away when he fired two rounds into the forehead of the guard, who dropped to the tarmac pavement like a drunken man. He then ran across to the two vehicles and using his special tool popped the doors, he then placed the grenades on the front seats and tied the string to the door handle. He returned to the corpse, fired two more rounds into the lock which freed the door, He dragged the dead body into the dimly lit room and dumped it on the floor. He turned on his torch and saw two large boxes that were open and displaying in full view many plastic bags full of a white substance.

The two boxes were nestled in some kind of straw presumably used for packing. He shone the torch around the storeroom and his eyes rested on a sign that said Benzine for motorboats not for vehicles, he unscrewed a Gerry can and spread the contents liberally around both boxes. Sam was just about ready to torch the place when a voice shouted 'Carlos, Carlos where the fuck are you?'. He wandered in to the storeroom and walked into a double tap to the face from a 9mm.

Sam backed away to the door and tossed a match into the Storeroom which erupted in flames. He closed the door and sprinted back to Luigi's re-entering the kitchen and then on to the restaurant.

'Lets go Chris', he said collecting a doggy bag from Luigi and dropping him a 10 dollar tip. They both moved swiftly through the kitchen and out the back door to a taxi with it's engine running.

'4240 5th Avenue please driver, lets get out of here.' said Sam

'OK Sam, how did it go', said Mary Jo who was driving the cab.

'It took me 9 minutes, 2 minutes over schedule, but better be safe than sorry' said Sam.

'What the hell are you doing here Mary Jo and where the hell did you get a taxi?', said Chris.

'We are a team are we not, the three of us and I got the cab from my brother in law', said Mary Jo. As they made their way northbound through Manhattan it was like world war three with fire engines, police and ambulances all rushing to the scene.

'Chris, please stay with me at the penthouse tonight there is plenty of room, you really don't want to be in the village tonight.

'OK' she said.

They reached 5th avenue said their goodnight to Mary Jo and took the elevator to the penthouse.

'It's not mine Chris, but I have some rich friends and I can stay hear as long as I like. I'll put the food in the oven and open up a bottle of Chablis.' he said.

'Turn on the TV and see if we caused a ruckus tonight', said Sam'.

The news girl was standing at the rear of the cafe Pacifico interviewing an FBI special agent.

'What is your take on this Special Agent?' she said

'My initial thoughts are that it is turf related, that is, I think the dead Cubans were trying to muscle in on Russian Mafia territory and the Russians took them out.'

'The drugs were completely destroyed in the fire, any residue is being analysed as we speak. Five men were killed, two being shot at point blank range, a typical hit by an assassin and three killed by an explosive device as they tried to escape the scene of the crime' he said.

The cameraman then focused on the glamorous presenter who said

'It doesn't look like the Cubans are going to do any business in New York, this is Sandra Derek from Greenwich Village returning you to the studio.'

'Supper's ready' Sam called from the kitchen and they both sat down to enjoy there belated dinner.

'I'm still in a state of shock, I've never ever been involved in a take down like that', said Chris. 'Lets just enjoy the rest of our meal and then I'll talk about it', said Sam.

They carried out the rest of the meal without any conversation, Sam topped up their glasses of Chablis, cleared the table and put the dishes in the cleaning machine. Then they both retired to the luxurious lounge. 'I'm not working at a hundred percent at the moment Sam, I'm sorry', said Chris.

'I overheard the gossip at the 52nd about your Senator Chris and that he can't keep his dick in his trousers. If you want to talk about it I'm a good listener', said Sam.

'I really thought that he was the one Sam', tears falling from her eyes.

Sam put his arm around her and she held on to him tears still streaming down her face. Finally, after twenty minutes or so she said 'Which way to the bathroom, Sam?', Sam pointed in the general direction and she was gone, She emerged a few minutes later more or less back to normal and sat down next to him on the sofa.

'I've seen enough tonight to realise that you are not a cop, so Samuel Collins who and what the hell are you?' she said.

'You got the name right Sam Collins, a cop, as you suggested I am not, I work for the U.S. secret service and I take my orders directly from a General in the Pentagon', said Sam. 'I used you and Mary Jo to help track down the Cubans, which I might add was very impressive. My brief was to destroy the Cubans effort to establish a market in New York and with you two we have managed to do just that', Sam concluded.

'A moment please, Chris', he said removing the phone from it's cradle and dialing the General's number.

'Good evening General, mission complete sir' said Sam.

'Good job, pass on my thanks to Sergeant Stacey and Detective Bonetti for their wonderful input', said the General. 'You can get your tail off to California Sam and I'll make contact with your next assignment'. He said.

'I would like to stay in New York and work with the two Detectives for a while if I may sir', said Sam.

'Permission granted, goodbye Sam, good job'. Said the General, replacing the telephone in it's cradle.

'I'd like to look into the so called Washington assassins case in more detail, I believe the FBI profiler's have got it all wrong. It's just a hunch at the moment Chris' he said.

'What would you like me to do?' said Chris,

'I would like you to go to the pathology lab and talk to the guy that carried out the autopsy on the guy that was shot in the Bronx and try to determine which way he was facing when he bought the bullet and where the bullet entered and exited his skull, I'm looking for an angle here to try and determine the shooter's position,' said Sam'.

'If you could get on it tomorrow and then meet me and Mary Jo at the kill point later, say 11am?'

'Now Sarge, I want you to go to bed.' said Sam.

When Sam rolled out of bed in the morning Chris had already left for work. He phoned Mary Jo at the

52nd and arranged for her to pick him up on 5th. Twenty minutes later, she arrived outside Doc Li's place collected Sam and got underway to the killing spot in the Bronx.

'Chris told me that she's on her way to see Doctor Nancy Goldstein at the morgue, she carried out the post on Raymond Briggs the victim of the shooting.' said Mary Jo.

They arrived at the scene and had a general look around, Sam searching the surrounding buildings for an ideal shooting spot. The FBI report said the spot the shooter chose was the third floor of a block of redundant offices. Sam agreed with this but his hunch was that the killer was not so much a pro as the FBI predicted.

They went to a nearby cafe and took a coffee and waited for Chris to join them. Mary Jo waved to Chris as she got out of the Crown Victoria placing the police sign on the dash. She ordered coffee and sat down alongside Sam..

'What have you got Chris?' said Sam.

Chris pulled out a copious amount of paper and read out loud, 'The bullet entered Brigg's skull just above his left ear and exited his right cheek just above his upper jawline, so the angle you were looking for Sam is 32 degrees.'

Sam pulled an ordinance survey street map out of his brief case, placed a dot depicting the body location and using a protractor drew a line at 32 degrees to the edge of the paper. Two hundred yards away the red line entered a ten-story building between the third and fourth floor.

'Lets go take a look.' said Sam.

When they reached the location they found a disused car park with a notice saying "No Admittance. Dangerous" which they completely ignored. They climbed the stairway to the fourth floor and to Sam's disappointment found that there was no clear shot to the kill point.

'Lets try the third floor.' said Sam.

'Bingo, he could get a clear shot from here.' Sam said. Sam fished in his pocket and pulled out three pairs of plastic booties which they all put on. 'He rested his arm on the window ledge here', said Chris 'He has left some bits of fabric along the sill.' 'Bag it' said Sam. 'Shit, I've got a tissue here with what looks like a pubic hair in it and the guy has either a heavy cold or has had a hand job, it's either snot or seamen', said Chris. 'Bag it' Sam said again. 'Yes' yelled Mary Jo 'I've got the same thing, a latex glove covered in what looks like seamen' she said. They carried on searching for another hour and then returned to the cafe.

'Lets set out some guidance rules', said Sam, 'when we are in the 52nd and out on day to day police work Chris is in charge, when we are engaged on the Briggs killing I'm the "Gaffer", are we clear?' said Sam. Both the girls nodded in agreement.

Chapter 30

'Lets get back to the precinct I need to talk to the Captain' said Sam. Chris phoned the precinct and set up an appointment for Sam and they left the area. 'Thanks for seeing me Captain' said Sam. I'm going to have to trust you one hundred percent sir', he said. 'You may not like what I'm going to do here', Sam continued.'

'The Cuban drug hit last night was nothing to do with the FBI, although they will probably try to take the credit, it was carried out by Sergeant Stacey, Mary Jo Bonetti and myself'. My cover here Captain is a UK cop here to observe only, but in truth I work for the U.S. Secret Service working out of the Pentagon. If you wish, I can give you a number to phone for verification', said Sam.

'I've been talking to Stacey on a daily basis about you, Sam and everything is good, your secret is safe with me', said the Captain.

'I think the FBI profile on the Briggs and other killings is way offline and given a few days can do an accurate re-write. I need the two ladies full time for one to two weeks, any chance Captain?', said Sam.

'Lets review it in one week Sam and see where we are at, you have the detectives full time for that week'.

'Thank you sir' said Sam and left the office.

He packed and posted the evidence bags-to the MI5 offices in London and attached a note to the Commander. '*Can you extract any DNA for any of the enclosed items? It's very important as it's regarding the Washington DC killer.*' Signed Colonel Sam Lassiter.

He met with the two detectives back at the 52nd and told them that he has a visitor from England coming over to view some paintings at Sotherby's. 'We can meet up on Monday and I may have some important info.'

He wished the girls a nice weekend and a well done for the days work at the kill site. He took a cab to Idlewild airport and sat down in the arrival area to wait for Lady Janet Templeton. The system announced the arrival of the BOAC flight from London and within five minutes the passengers were coming through the gate. Then, there she was a vision of beauty, grace and elegance gliding her way along the red carpet like a model on a runway.

'Samuel, lovely to see you' she said 'Close your mouth',

'I'm sorry Ma'am I must have been affected by this vision of beauty before me', said Sam.

'I'm just an old lady trying to hang on to some threads of youth', she said.

'And winning too', said Sam. Ushering her towards the taxi rank. They finally boarded a taxi and headed for Manhattan and the penthouse on 5th Avenue. He helped with Janet's luggage and let her into her room where she unpacked and got herself organised. Sam then made the phone call to General Richards.

'Sir I need to get into the military recruitment offices in DC, can you help? Next Tuesday would be good', said Sam.

'No problem it will be done, just turn up Sam, are you on to something good?' said the General.

'Not sure, but it could be and you will be the first to know sir', he said.

'I think it would be a good idea for you to stay in this evening and get yourself organized on New York time, what do you think?' said Sam. 'I'll put a couple of easy meals in the oven and we can wash it down with a bottle of your favourite Chianti', he said.

'That sounds good, Sam', she said turning on the shower at full blast.

Janet came out of her room to join Sam in the kitchen, she was dressed in a full length white towel dressing gown and white fluffy slippers. Sam had already changed into a tee shirt and shorts.

'Can we forget the Lady Janet and the Ma'am thing, please call me Janet' she said.

'OK I can do that', said Sam.

After the meal they both sat on the huge white sofa and sipped their Chianti. Sam was aware of her closeness and the smell of expensive perfume and body lotion. 'Are you OK with Italian food Janet? asked Sam. 'Love it' came the reply from Janet. Sam picked up the phone and dialed Luigi's and reserved a table for two for tomorrow at 8pm, before putting the phone down Luigi said 'The table is reserved for you Sam but no bonfires and fireworks' 'Not even a sparkler' said Sam, 'One more thing, are you bringing that pretty detective with you?' asked Luigi. 'No I'm not Luigi I'm bringing Miss England' said Sam.

'What a disappointment Luigi is going to have when a handsome young man walks into his place with an old lady', said Janet.

'He will adore you Janet, a forty six year old not looking a day over twenty five.', 'Now you are telling "Porkies", she said, and started walking to her bedroom. 'Are you looking at my bum Colonel?' she said

'Yep' said Sam. She continued on her way to her room with a little wiggle and giggle. After five minutes she returned to the lounge and sat down close to Sam. 'I'm going to take another shower, I still feel a little grubby from the trip.'

'Give me a yell when you are through and I'll follow you in', said Sam. A couple of minutes later, Sam heard the sound of water hitting the side of the shower cubical. Five minutes later all quiet.

'Shower's free!' Janet called out.

Sam gave her a little time to vacate the shower and then moved slowly to the bathroom, he passed the misted up shower cubical, took off his clothes and opened the cubical door. There she was completely naked with water running down her beautiful body. She took a pace forward and put both arms around him, Sam held her very close and planted a passionate kiss on her waiting lips, both sets of tongues were in action.

After what seemed to be an endless kiss they parted, Sam let his hand wander to her ample breasts and her erect nipples. Janet let out a little groan as she sank to her knees, her mouth only a few inches away from Sam's massive hard-on. She took hold of Sam's manhood and gently eased her mouth down the whole length of his penis. After Janet had gone to work on his rock hard penis, it didn't take long for Sam to explode and shoot semen all over Janet's face.

'I'm so sorry Janet, It's been a long time.'

'Nothing to worry about Sam I enjoyed every minute, thank you' she said. They turned on the shower again and enjoyed washing each others backs.

'I'm glad you came when you did, my knees were killing me on that tiled floor' she laughed.

Sam looked down at his still semi hard penis and said 'When are you going to learn how to behave yourself?'

They sat together on the sofa for the next hour or so scanning the Sotherby's auction catalogue,

'Lets get to Sotherby's around about 9am, this will give us plenty of time to view the paintings and I can tick off the pictures I will be bidding for.' said Janet.

'Sounds like a plan.' said Sam.

He continued by saying 'I'm no expert Janet, but those city-scapes by Herman Rose and the portraits by Fay Klienman are fantastic. But my pride and joy would be to own a Rothko abstract, I was talking to an art expert in California just before I left and he thinks the Rothko's would sell high', said Sam.

'I agree Sam I did some research myself before I left the UK, change of subject, I think I'll go shopping do you want to come with me?' Said Janet.

'Not a good idea Janet, New York is not a good place to go shopping after dark, a lot of "nutters" about, anyway, I've already put a couple of lasagne in the oven and have opened a bottle of Chianti to breathe a little.

'OK, I'll be back in 10, just going to freshen up a little', she said.

Sam prepared the two places at the table and poured two glasses of wine. A few minutes later Janet came into the kitchen wearing a tee shirt and tiny pink shorts.

It was also apparent that she wasn't wearing a bra; she stopped at the sink and dried a few items of cutlery. Sam walked up behind her and put his arms around her and gave her a squeeze.

'I feel you're enjoying my company', twitching her rear end and backing into Sam's groin.

'Again, you are a master of the understatement, moving his semi hard penis against her pink shorts.

'Get out of here and let me get on with my meal', she said with a laugh.

They ate their meal in relative silence and when completed placed all the dirty dishes in the machine, Sam buried himself in his program for the next few days and Janet continued to study the brochures of the Southerby's auction. Sam went to the kitchen to remove the crocks from the dishwasher and stack them in the cupboards, he returned to the lounge to find Janet fast asleep on the huge sofa.

He gently lifted her up and carried her to her bedroom and placed her in the bed and placed the cover over her, as she hit the pillow she said 'Sam I'm so sorry, but I think I'm falling in love with you.', before Sam could summon up an answer she had dosed off to sleep again.

The following morning they both showered and dressed and took a cab to Southerby's where Janet viewed the paintings and recorded the lot numbers of the paintings she would be bidding for. Four hours later they both left the auction rooms, Janet with a huge smile on her face. She had spent the best part of $80,000 and adding a further seven beautiful American masterpieces to her gallery.

They took a roundabout route to Manhattan, parked up and did some shopping, then returned to the Penthouse and relaxed again on the sofa. Janet made several phone calls just to ensure that the paintings were nicely packed for the journey to England, she checked with the carrier who informed her that every precaution had been taken for a damage free delivery to the UK, Janet then retired to her room to get ready for tonight's dinner at Luigi's.

Sam phoned Chris Stacey and Mary Jo Bonetti and gave them both the same message. 'Be ready to travel to DC on Monday, pack your bag for three days,' he said', I'm expecting a good result from the MI5 experts in London probably around midnight tonight, I'll put you both in the picture if the news is good.' said Sam.

Sam and Janet spent a quiet romantic night at Luigi's and left for 5th Avenue at about 11.30, they went straight to bed in Janet's room and fell asleep in each others arms. They woke up at 8am and both decided that they would spend the whole day in bed, making love several times. Janet was a very satisfied woman, and Sam for once proud of himself for not having premature ejaculation, maybe, he thought, that he had cracked it, but put it down to the beautiful person he was with.

The cab journey to La Guardia Airport was quiet and uneventful.

'Are you OK?' said Sam.

'I'm fine, although, I would prefer to stay in New York with you, than running off to Chicago to see a very distant relative.' Janet said.

'But duty calls' she said.

She got out of the cab and made her way to the departure lounge, on entering the door she turned waved and mouthed 'Love you'. Sam returned to the apartment sat down and waited for the important phone call from London, he turned on the TV and watched a fuzzy picture of a baseball match involving the Yankees at Shea stadium. He fell asleep and was woken at 2.30 am when the phone trembled in it's holder.

'Hello Sam Collins here',

'Sam it's Commander Lansbury MI5 I like your new name but prefer Colonel Lassiter', he said. 'Don't forget Sam that DNA is not 100% reliable and it's early days in the research, I think it will be many years before it becomes an actual science and remember it not admissible in a court of law,'

'I've got a report for you on the stuff you sent over, I've had my top people take a good long look at it, here's the bottom line', he said,

The fabric samples found on the window ledge are from a United States Infantry flak jacket, the tissue with semen and pubic hair found adjacent to the shooters position are from a black person, the 30 Caliber spent cartridge with clear thumb and forefinger prints on it we think are from the shooter, the discarded latex glove also contained semen from the shooter, but the latent print we got from the inside of the latex glove was not the shooters. It seems you have two homosexual black men who have this sexual ritual just before or just after a kill', he concluded.

'A wonderful job, thank you so much Commander', said Sam.

'Take care of yourself Colonel', he said replacing the phone in it's holder.

He left a message on Chris Stacey and Mary Jo's answer service to the effect that we are a go for tomorrow. The following morning with Mary Jo driving, they set off for Washington DC, each one hundred miles taking turns at the wheel. Seven hours later they stopped at a nice clean looking motel approximately 30 miles from DC and checked in, as soon as Sam reached his room he phoned the FBI in Washington DC and asked to be put through to the Agent In Charge responsible for the 'Washington Killers'.

'Which one do you want sir? We have a dozen agents on the case', she said.

'I want to talk to somebody capable of keeping there mouth shut sweetie' he said.

'One moment sir',

A new voice broke the musical interlude and said, 'My name is Special Agent In charge David Sinclair, how may I help you?'

'You can help me by turning off the record button and promise me that you are not trying to trace this call.' said Sam,

'It's done.' came the reply.

'My name is Sam Collins and I work for the United States Secret Service based at the Pentagon, if and when we meet I'll give you a phone number to verify this,' he continued. 'The profile the FBI issued to all the police departments on the East coast is basically a load of rubbish and I can pick many holes in it.'

'What I would like you to do David is to come and see me and my two detectives from NYPD at the Jefferson Motel on route 66 as soon as possible'. 'If you have recorded this call and if you are followed to this location I will abort the meeting, are we clear David?',

'Crystal, I'll see you within the hour, traffic permitting.' he said.

Sam laid all the information on his desk then went off to join the girls at the bar. 'Anybody hungry?, I'm starving!' said Sam.

'Lets eat!' said Mary Jo.

Sam told them about his call with David Sinclair at Washington FBI and said that he would be joining them for a meeting in the next half hour, 'This guy is one of the Agents In Charge dealing with the Washington killers and,' he added 'I think he can be trusted.'

David Sinclair arrived and went directly to the receptionist who pointed him in the direction of the dining area, Sam gave him a wave and beckoned him over to their table and he shook hands with all three of them. He was typical FBI, smart suit and polished shoes and short well coiffured hair.

'This is Sergeant Chris Stacey and this is Mary Jo Bonett from NYPD, my team, and my name is Sam Collins.' he said.

'David Sinclair FBI' he said.

'Are you hungry David?' said Mary Jo,

'I'm good thanks', he replied.

They finished their meal and adjourned to Sam's room.

Sam began 'The information the FBI profiler's provided to the various police departments on the East coast was as I have already told you, a load of old crap!', Davids head dropped a little. 'The killers are not white highly effective marksmen, they are black and not particularly bright when it comes to selecting a suitable sniping position.' 'As far as the Bronx shooting was concerned, they got that wrong as well!' said Sam.

'We have evidence that the two perp's are black homosexuals who have this perverse ritual every time they commit a kill. We have to know if you will work with us and not blab it around the FBI until we put it to bed.', said Sam.

'You have my word.' said David.

'We now come to the point where we run out of factual evidence and we are into a bit of a 'hunch' situation.', said Sam.

'I believe that the shooter is a guy that has been rejected by the military and is trying to show everybody that he is an Audie Murphy' said Sam.

'I have arranged an appointment with the Central Army Recruitment people in DC, we are to be there at 10.30 tomorrow morning, prepare yourself for a long day searching through files.' 'I'll leave you guys now, I have a few calls to make and by the way David if you want to check me out I can give you a number at the Pentagon', said Sam.

'Not needed' said David. With a hand shake Sam left the Dining Area.

At 10am the next day they arrived at the Military Recruitment Head Office in Washington very close to the FBI building on 10th Avenue. They were greeted by a tiny figure of a young lady who directed them to her office.

'I'm Tessa Sanderson and I'm here to give toy all the help I can,' she said. 'I've had a head start on you guys as General Richards pointed me in the right direction.' she said.

On her office table were a whole lot of files, in all sorts of colours, Red, Pink, White, Grey and Blue,

'OK the red ones are black women, the pink files are white women' she said.

'Lose the women Tessa and the white males' said Sam.

'That leaves us with 152 probables.' said Tessa stacking the files in a pile in the centre of her table.

'OK, grab 25 files each and look for any refusals on grounds of' homosexual activity.' said Sam.

The room went quiet as everybody gave 100% to the search, any dubious or strange refusals were placed in the middle of the table. After an hour the final file was discarded on the no interest pile.

'That leaves us with six' said Tessa. Sam had invited Lieutenant Mike Withers from MPDC to attend with one of his detectives. Sam handed the paperwork over from his Captain at NYPD, this was confirmation that the two police forces would be working together on this bust.

'OK, Chris and David take the two on the East side of town, Mike and Ted take the one down town and the one to the North. I'll take the two to the South with Mary Jo.'

'If it's OK with Tessa we meet back here at 10am tomorrow', said Sam. Tessa nodded an OK.

'So lets do it!' said Sam.

Stakeouts were probably the worst bit of Police work but it had to be done and all three teams were in position ready for the long vigil. Ten in the morning six tired faces sat opposite Sam fanning through their paperwork, Mike reported that one of the suspects was now happily married with two kids and was into real estate and the other guy had left his wife two years ago and she didn't know and didn't want to know where he was.

Chris reported that one of her suspects had left the area and the other had joined the Fire Service, unfortunately he had died in a fire one year ago,

Sam stood up and said 'I think we've got the bastards!' 'they both arrived home at midnight holding hands, the little guy dancing along the street like a Russian Ballet Dancer. Mary Jo gave it twenty minutes or so and approached the van that was parked at the rear of there walk-up. She scraped the paint off the rear of the vehicle to reveal that the van had received a poor spray job, the white was showing through in places.'

'They've got to be the prime suspects.' said Sam.

'I've set up a Marine cordon and search and destroy system for us to nail these perps', said Sam.

'Chris, Mary Jo Ted and Mike will do the entry, bust the two of them, cuff them and read them there rights, Mike's second Guy will cover the van and the third guy will cover the old Ford at the front of the building in case they try to run for it.' 'David will go with the entry team purely as an observer. When the entry team has made the bust, Chris will make the call to me and I'll get the place crawling with MPDC and FBI Personnel, and let the forensic people earn their money.' said Sam.

'One more thing, Chris take some photo's of the inside of the apartment, lots of photo's OK' said Sam.

OK 1am, We go!, now get some rest'. Said Sam.

At 1am everybody was in position and the MPDC and the FBI were standing by, Chris and Mike smashed the door down and both shouted clear on passing the sitting room, they burst into the bedroom and turned on the light.

'Nobody move! Nobody move!' said Chris as Mary Jo and Ted entered the bedroom.

'Don't hurt us' yelled the little guy, as they slowly got out of the bed in there vests and shorts.

'On the floor' Chris yelled, they rolled on their fronts and as Mary Jo and Ted cuffed them she read them their rights.

She and Ted together with David had a good look around the squalid living room, comics, the 'Sniper' magazine and various homosexual magazines. Then they both spotted the Springfield Rifle propped against the wall with several boxes of thirty caliber bullets, she took plenty of photographs and phoned Sam on his cumbersome portable phone that the mission was a success.

Sam called in the troops from the MPDC and the FBI and within five minutes the place was alive with yellow, red and blue lights. The 'Paddy Wagon' lock-up arrived and the two perp's were frog marched roughly through the haze and into the back of the wagon, where they were placed into leg irons. With the prisoners safely locked away, Chris and Mike finished writing their reports and the whole team sat and relaxed in the detectives room in down town DC.

Sam called David to one side and said 'I hope you are going to be alright playing second fiddle to a bunch of ordinary cops'

'I'll be fine and you are not ordinary cops, it's been a pleasure working with you' said David.

'Please remember the arrests were made jointly by two officers from NYPD and two officers from MPDC, with a back-up crew from two other officers from MPDC and a Special Agent In Charge from the FBI over seeing things. Do not refer to me in any reports other than a 'Detective On Loan' from the London Met in the UK.' Sam said.

They were all sitting at a table drinking coffee when Sam said 'We will be leaving for New York tomorrow just after lunch if that's OK Mike?'

'Not a problem', said Mike.

'If you guys can make it we will be eating at the diner adjacent to the motel at 12 noon tomorrow and the FBI is picking up the bill!' said Sam.

It was 4am when they got back to the Jefferson motel and everybody apart from Sam went to bed. Sam went to the lobby and made two calls, one to England to thank the Commander for the info and one to the General to inform him that they nailed the Washington shooters and that he would be returning to Santa Barbara on Sunday to spend Christmas in the sun.

Twelve noon on the dot Sam, Chris, Mary Jo and David from the FBI entered the diner to find Mike and the three MPDC cops already inside waiting for us.

'Don't get a "Freebie" from a "Feebee" to often' said Mike.

When the meal ended Sam addressed all the team and said 'It's been a pleasure working with a bunch of professionals and I have informed my boss at the Pentagon of that fact. He will be writing to the Chief of Police in both New York and Washington, recommending commendations for you all and well deserved I might add!' 'I'm leaving to spend Christmas in Santa Barbara next Sunday, but I would very much like to treat you all to dinner in New York on Saturday, say 8pm at my favourite Italian restaurant Luigi's in Greenwich village, please try and make it, bring your wives or lady friends along'. Said Sam. 'Mike, call me with numbers later in the week.'

They said their goodbyes and Sam noticed that Chris and David were really getting along well and David gave her a little hug as she was about to leave. This will be good for Chris at this time thought Sam.

They shared the driving duties on the way back to New York and made it back inside seven hours.

'I'm taking tomorrow off ladies to catch up with my correspondence, I'll see you Thursday at the 52nd", said Sam as he slowly climbed out of the hired motor and entered 4240 Fifth Avenue, took the elevator to the penthouse and just about made it to the sofa before collapsing in a heap, he slept soundly until lunchtime the following day.

On the Thursday morning Sam stopped off at Grazianno's for a coffee and an egg sandwich only to find Chris and Mary Jo already there.

'Good morning ladies, how are you today?' said Sam.

'We're fine Sam how about you?', said Chris.

'I'm good', he said.

They all travelled across the street and entered the 52nd precinct and were greeted with loud cheers and thunderous hand clapping from what seemed to be the whole of the 52nd, leading the applause was the precinct Captain who was obviously elated and very proud of his two lady detectives. Sam pulled back and ushered Chris and Mary Jo forward and joined in the applause for them. The two girls wouldn't let him get away with this and beckoned him forward to join them. After much patting on the back and hand shakes finally the detectives room reverted to normal.

Chris and Mary Jo sat down and sorted today's itinerary while Sam stood by sipping some coffee, just before they left Crisis's phone rang, it was Mike saying that all four would be showing up on Saturday with their wives.

'That's great! Look forward to seeing you!' said Chris, She turned to Sam and said 'The guys and their wives are up for the dinner at Luigi's on Saturday Sam and by the way, David called me at home and said that he would be pleased to come along.' Sam gave her a knowing look.

'What?' said Chris.

Chapter 31

The Captain's office door opened and out walked the Mayor of New York, the NYPD Chief of Police followed by the 52nd Precinct's Captain. The detectives room went silent as the captain introduced the Mayor who's speech was a general well done to all the officers of the 52$^{nd.}$

The Chief of Police was not short in praise for Sargent Stacey and Detective Bonetti who *'both excelled in good solid police work, flare and tenacity to bring help bring down the two killers from Washington'*.

He asked Chris and Mary Jo to step forward to receive the highest award available to a serving member of the police force.

Chris and Mary Jo rose from their seats to a huge roar from the other detectives and walked across the room straight passed the Chief of Police and both gave Sam a huge long hug.

They both whispered 'Thank you.' and stood to attention in front of the Chief of Police to except their medals. The beer cans popped and the girls were lost in the crowd of well wishers.

Sam was slipping quietly away when he was stopped by the precinct Captain 'Where the hell are you going Sam?', 'It's your party as well',

'Not a party goer Cap', your girls did you proud, go and enjoy the moment', said Sam.

The Captain gave him a parting shot and said 'I enjoyed working with you Sam although we did bend a few rules, take good care of yourself!'

Sam returned to the penthouse to find a package from Commander Lansbury, he opened it up to find a comprehensive report on all the findings at the kill site. He re-directed the parcel and added a note to David Sinclair saying that the contents could help convict the two perpetrators and move them closer to the electric chair. '*PS. I know you've got the hots for Chris, take it nice and slow David, she has just been hurt very badly. Look forward to seeing you on Saturday.*'

He rushed down to reception and got the U.S. Postal service to collect the package for special delivery.

He returned to the lounge and sat at the under used desk and turned on the table lamp. He was just about to call the general when the phone rang and it was Mary Jo.

'We have a full house for Saturday, the two back-up lads from MPDC are already on the road here, they are going to make a weekend of it, the girls are going shopping and the lads are going to have a few beers, David has asked Chris if she would go with him and she said yes, and I will be with my husband Henry.'

'Mike and Ted are flying in tomorrow with their wives, it should be a great night!'

'The only person without an escort is you Sam.'

'I'm good, I'm bringing a 46 year English old biddy, they do have wheelchair access at Luigi's don't they' said Sam tongue in cheek.

'She's called Janet and she has been looking forward to meeting you and Chris'.

After he has finished talking to Mary Jo, he called the General and told him that he was spending Christmas in Santa Barbara and to use the boat address for any correspondence.

'I'm hearing some good things about the Washington business and the grapevine has it that you masterminded the whole "Shebang" Sam, you have given us a lot of kudos by nailing these two. The top man at the White House has been informed and is very pleased, have a good holiday Sam.'

He called the airline at La Guardia to confirm Janet's ETA from Chicago and then booked a flight to Los Angeles for Monday morning. His last call was to Studio Monique where he left a message on her answer phone that his arrival time was 5pm on Monday next.

Janet arrived back in New York at 11.30am and Sam was there to greet her and after a quick hug took a cab to 5th Avenue.

'I had a nice trip, but it's nice to see you again Sam', said Janet,

'What have you been up to while I was away?' she said.

'The operation to take down the two shooters from Washington was a complete success both Chris and Mary Jo were outstanding, so were the guys from the Metropolitan Police DC' said Sam.

'They are safely locked up in DC now and will more than likely get the chair', said Sam.

'Tell me about Chicago, did you like it Janet?'

'The North side was lovely, but it frightened me to death driving through the South side' said Janet.

'Tonight we are having a little celebration party at a restaurant called Luigi's, many people say it's the best in town. The whole crew that were responsible for taking down the Washington shooters will be there, fourteen of us, you have no idea how wonderful I will feel walking into that restaurant with you on my arm especially if you wear that little black dress', said Sam. 'Both Chris and Mary Jo are really looking forward to meeting you.'

'I'll wear the little black number if you wear that lovely Italian suit', said Janet.

'Deal' said Sam.

Chapter 32

They took a cab to Luigi's and were the last to arrive. Chris leaned over and whispered in Sam's ear

'Some old biddy you've got there Sam, she is absolutely gorgeous!'

Everybody introduced themselves and they all enjoyed a wonderful meal. You could see the class come out in the way Janet handled the various conversations, she came across as a perfect English lady, which of course she was.

'David rose from his seat and said

'A Toast!' 'It's been a pleasure working with you Sam.' The whole party raised their glasses towards Sam.

'As Janet knows, my knowledge of the English language is somewhat limited, but one thing I do know is that I've never had a better bunch to work with and, we got the "Buggers!". said Sam.

As the romantic Italian music filtered through Luigi's P A system the talking was restricted and people were chatting in little groups.

'Are you just here in the U.S. For a holiday trip?' Chris asked Janet.

'It was a rushed trip really Chris, Sam wrote to me and told me about an art auction at Southerby's New York and after looking at the brochure decided that I needed to come over and do some bidding', said Janet.

'I have an art gallery at my home in England and to have some very famous American paintings hanging on my walls would be fantastic' she said.

'If you ever come to England Chris you must come and stay with us at the Manor',

'I would love that!' said Chris.

'Sam is an old friend of my family, he was my son's best man at his wedding and he made a friend of my husband Sir Keith Templeton and not many people can do that', she laughed.

It got to 11.30 and Sam paid the bill and after a lot of hugging and kissing all parties went their different ways.

'I'll see you the next time I'm in New York Luigi' said Sam,

'OK, but no fires or loud bangs', said Luigi laughing out loud.

Sam took Janet's hand and they thumbed down a cab. 'Gillies West' driver please', said Sam.

'Where are you taking me Samuel?'

'I'm taking you dancing Lady Templeton, something I missed out on at your Son's wedding.'

They danced together until the early hours and Sam was feeling a little horny so he pulled away slightly from her.

'Why are you dancing so far away from me?' she said

'I've got a massive hard on and I'll probably pole vault you across the dance floor', said Sam

'Oh so you have you naughty boy!' and pulled him in very close gently grinding her hips into his crutch area.

'Are you sure you can't dance any closer Sam?', she said,

'If I dance any closer I'll be dancing behind you' said Sam.

After Janet having had such a wonderful time in America, it was obvious how the night out was going to end. Both Sam and Janet couldn't get enough of each other.

They arrived back at 5th Avenue and went straight to their respective rooms and changed, Janet in a white flowing dressing gown and Sam in a T-shirt and boxer shorts.

'Make it good for me Sam it's got to last a long time' She said

For the first time since he set foot in the USA, looking down he said,

'You heard what the lady said, so don't let me down Mr. Pecker'.

They both got into bed completely naked, Janet holding Sam very close. A few moments later she eased her way over Sam's body and straddled him. He felt the damp pubic hair run over his lower stomach as she worked her way slowly up his body. She continued to weave her way up Sam's body, over his chest then stopped just above his mouth, where she opened herself up and lowered herself gently down on Sam. Although Sam had seen pictures of this activity in thrown away porno mag's in gentlemen's toilets, he had never participated before. He got busy with his tongue like an old pro and soon Janet was writhing in ecstasy as Sam teased both the rough and the smooth side of her clitoris.

When Janet raised her hips from Sam and shimmied down to Sam's erection she lifted it vertically and lowered herself on to it, soon developing a slow sensual rhythm.

The love making went on for what seemed to be the sexual journey of a lifetime.

'I can't hold on much longer Janet'.

'You don't have to darling Sam', she said, increasing the tempo of her lovemaking. There were a lot of "oohs and Ahs" when the both climaxed together.

Janet collapsed on top of Sam leaving his semi hard manhood still inside her.

'Close your eyes Sam and rest, lets enjoy the sticky time', she said as they both fell asleep completely satisfied.

In the morning Sam woke up to find the bed empty on Janet's side, a note on the bedside table with an S on the front.

Darling Sam;

I'm not too good at goodbyes so it's best I leave without any tears or fuss. You have shown me a magical time in New York and I will miss you and my new friends at NYPD. Please be assured that I won't do anything stupid or irrational, but I'm sure that you already know that I have fallen in love with you.

I shall return to the UK to my wonderful family and try to bring a little happiness to Keith and help nurse him through his current illness.

If you manage to get over to the UK this summer to watch some cricket, please call in and see us at the Manor.

Love Janet xxx

Sam showered and changed, cleaned the entire apartment, called a cab and was on his way to La Guardia Airport.

Chapter 33

It was 10.30 when the plane touched down in LA. He made his way through passport control and customs into the arrival hall.

There she was waving to him as though there was no lost tomorrow and not in tatty cut-offs and a T-shirt, but in a figure clutching white jump suit, looking like a million dollars.

'Taxi sir?' said Monique,

'Spud you look sensational!' said Sam.

During the ride home to Santa Barbara she didn't stop talking about Studio Monique and the incredible beginning to her business career.

'I am now contract signed to be the official photographer for the whole of David Bergman's Companies. I will be a millionaire within a year'! she said.

She dropped Sam off at the marina, Sam slowly got out of the jeep.

'You look totalled', she said,

'Got it in one, those tough New Yorkers', said Sam.

'Have a nice rest and come over to the house on Christmas day.' 'My brother, some of his surgeons and their wives will be coming for lunch and drinks.'

'David and Samantha and of course me will make up the party.'

Sam spent the next two days relaxing on the luxury cruiser, writing letters to Janet, Lance, Katherine and Trisha, and hoping and praying no registered letters arrived from the Pentagon.

Christmas Day morning he drove up to Jonny's beautiful house that was tucked nicely into the soft flowing hills of Santa Barbara. Doctor John Li's house was typical of the rich and famous a house that would be well suited for a Hollywood movie star. It was a huge Mexican rancho type structure painted white with two swimming pools, one inside and one out, seven bedrooms, a massive lounge overlooking the Santa Barbara coastline. The huge bay windows overlooking beautiful tropical gardens.

He spent most of the morning with Manuel who was tending the lovely flowers that surrounded the property. They both slowly drifted back towards the house Sam going to the lounge and Manuel to the kitchen to help with the Christmas Day meal.

Sam was sitting next to a huge bay window which gave a panasonic view of down own Santa Barbara and the bay area.

'All this because you believed in me', Said Jonny Li

'I was right was I not "John Jo", said Sam.

They both sat on one of the massive sofas and Sam looked towards his Doctor friend and said,

'When I sit and listen to you and your medics talking I don't understand half of what you are talking about' said Sam 'I just try to nod my head at the right time'.

'I've been in the killing game to long, I must get out of the business and try to give rather than take away.

'Like what Sam, can I help in any way?' said Dr. Li.

'Maybe there is, I've always had this fascination to be in anesthetics' said Sam.

'Where the hell did that come from?' said the Doctor.

'I've always been fascinated by operation theaters and I'm clearly not bright enough to be a surgeon, then why not go for the next best thing' said Sam.

'You are very serious about this?' said Jonny,

'Very!' said Sam.

Doctor John picked up the telephone and spoke to some obviously important person, the conversation went on for ten minutes. After completing several laps of his lounge with his phone stuck to his ear he said 'Many thanks Charles, I'll be in touch'.

'A CRNA course started way back last October, you will join the class on Monday 14th January 1946, you have a lot of work to do to catch up with the other students who have a terms start on you', said Dr.John. 'It's a degree course to become a Certified Registered Nurse Anesthetics (CRNA}. 'You will be trained to be responsible for managing and monitoring a patients pain levels and vital information during medical and surgical procedures', said the Doctor.

'Thanks once again John' said Sam.

'Welcome to the wonderful world of medicine'! said the Doctor.

After a beautifully prepared lunch everybody sat around the lounge and handed out the presents. Sam gave the Doctor a stethoscope with solid silver fittings and for Monique two modern art paintings for her studio. He bought two racing cars for Manuel's two boys, Sam received a lovely pair of the latest running shoes from Monique and some running socks from Manuel's boys.

'I will give you my present tomorrow at lunch on the "John Jo", it was to heavy for me to carry', said the Doctor.

The following day all the gang turned up for the lunch which Manuel had prepared in the Galley. They all sat down at the table and Manuel started serving.

'Merry Christmas my good friend', said Doctor John passing over a load of documents all referring to he luxury cruiser.

'I told you the present was to heavy for me to handle didn't I', he continued. The "John Jo" is now all yours.'

Sam left the boats main lounge and went up to the flying bridge a few tears running down his face. He turned to wipe down his eyes only to find Monique a few paces away looking at him.

'Nobody has been so kind to me as the Li family has, I just don't believe it', Monique moved over towards him and gave him a prolonged hug, 'You made it possible for me and my brother to have a life, we are just returning a favour' she said giving him a sisterly kiss.

Chapter 34

Sam attended the Induction on the 14th January, at Santa Barbara County General Hospital situated 3 miles west of the City. The Hospital was framed by Calle Road, San Antonia Road and the aptly named Camino Del Remedio (Way of Remedy) and was guided through the next terms work load.

It was explained to him that he would be attending Santa Barbara General and his agenda would be Mondays and Tuesdays general nursing duties on the wards or theatre under supervision, Wednesdays, all day lectures in the training centre, Thursdays home study day reviewing the weeks subjects and Fridays the training centre again to sit test papers, the results of which will be recorded for continuous assessment.

The Senior Nurse who conducted the Induction said that Doctor Li had informed her that he may be called away from time to time on government business, but with course notes could catch up especially as he would be providing extra tuition for you. The course is normally of two years duration, but due to your time out probably nearer three for you.

'If I might suggest Mr. Collins you put the hard work in the first year to Physiology and Chemistry and the following year to Physics, Anatomy and Biochemistry', she said.

Sam returned to the boat and started to browse through some of the books that the Doctor had left for him. He phoned the Two Star at the Pentagon and explained his present situation.

'I've got to get out of the killing business sir, I'm getting a bit "Bomb Happy"' said Sam. 'I would very much like to complete a degree course sir, but it would need a time out of two years', said Sam.

'You have done wonders for me and the Secret Service Sam and the person at the White House is more than happy with your results. I'll tell you what I'll do, I'll put you on reserve back-up duties which compared with what you have been doing will seem very lightweight, but it will ensure that you have plenty of time off for your studies. I'll drop your salary to $25 000 retainer, what do you say to that young Sam?'

'Thank you so much sir', said Sam.

He relaxed and wrote letters to Janet, Lance and Trisha telling his news that he was starting a degree course in January to qualify for a fully qualified anesthetist.

Everything was quiet, no wires from the Pentagon and Sam thought he could get used to being a student. He just wished that Lance were in the area to assist him in his studies. As well as a full day under supervision on Tuesdays and Wednesdays, Sam enrolled in further education evening classes to assist in his efforts to catch up with the rest of the class of twenty five trainees. So there it was, all set up and ready to go.

There were twenty five trainees in the group only six male students, so Sam slipped quietly into the back row of the class trying not to draw much attention to himself. The lectures were well presented and he enjoyed every single minute in class. The bell sounded spot on 9pm and the session finished with the instructor handing out notes and areas that needed more study.

Sam climbed in his MG and drove slowly out of the Hospital car park, he turned left and spotted one of his class mates standing at a bus stop.

'Need a ride?' said Sam.

'Great I've just missed my bus' she said.

'Climb in' said Sam.

They drove at a steady pace the MG's motor purring.

'Where do you want to go Nurse?' said Sam.

'It's only a couple of miles but it's an awkward place to get to and by the way, my name is Jill McGuire' she said.

'I'm Sam, Sam Collins.'

Two miles or so further on she pointed out her little Condo 'here we are and thanks, Sam' she said.

'Are you attending night school on Thursdays Jill?' said Sam.

'Yes I am'

'OK here's my card, give me a call if you need a ride' said Sam. Sliding the gear into first and smoothly pulling away.

Sam returned to his beautiful now owned home took a quick glance at the class notes and put them in a file marked "Study" on Thursday. Wednesdays we were more or less supervised all day, Sam spent most of the day cleaning the anesthetic gear and getting familiar with the various dials and feeder lines. He couldn't wait to get the call from the operating theatre.

Sam sat down at his large table in the lounge and had paper spread all over it as he started his first day long study day. At 9.30 am his phone rang it was Jill,

'Hey Sam I'll take you up on your offer of a ride to evening class tonight if that's OK?' she said.

'Not a problem I'll see you at 5.30' said Sam.

Sam arrived at Jill's condo and she was standing outside ready to go her arms full of books and notes. Sam sat in his normal seat in class and just before the lecture began she moved in alongside Sam.

'Maybe we can work together?' she said shyly.

'I'd like that' said Sam.

The Chemistry package was supposed to be an easy ride, so the lecturer said that he would like to close out this and move on to the more demanding physics. Sam studied hard with Jill's help through the whole of January hopefully retaining enough to at least get a 'C' in his first test.

A letter arrived from his Auntie Hilda saying that his mum had passed on 13th January quietly and peacefully and happy to join all her friends in heaven. Auntie Hilda took care of the funeral arrangements and thanked Sam for all the money he had sent over in the last couple of years.

'The next time you are in the UK pop down and see me and we will go and visit your mum's little plaque.'

Sam wiped a stray tear from his eye and went back to his studies trying to concentrate. John had laid on one of his nurses to assist him in his studies, so Sam invited Jill to the extra sessions with nurse Mason. Susan Mason was a typical nurse that any plastic surgeon would employ, tall, attractive and just the type that the older ladies would like to look like. One would be mistaken if they classed her as a dumb blonde, this lady new her stuff.

Sam dreaded the first test paper but managed to get through it with a pass and a 'C-'.

The first set back came with a wire from the Pentagon.

Hello Sam,

sorry to go back on my word to you but I have a problem, I've lost two of my guys last week down in Bogota, they didn't make it out. As from now you are on full status and full salary".

'*The Ku Klux Klan are getting to big for their boots again Sam, they are enjoying a surge in recruitment, we need you to go to Memphis and Knoxville and slow down the inductions.*

They are stringing up negro's and causing chaos to black neighborhoods going around wearing long white nightshirts and stupid head gear, they seem to like setting fire to crosses as well.'

'*I want you to go to Memphis and even up the numbers a little Sam, I don't care how you do it it's your call.''*

I have enclosed an open return ticket LA to Memphis international along with intel of the top "honcho's" of the Klan in the area.'

'*Your cover for the project is to assist a professor who is writing a book on our allies' activities in WW2 in Burma.' 'His name is Henry Langsdale'.*

'*Wire me with your requirements to clean this mess up Sam.'*

Sam put together a list:

Sniper Rifle
Silencer/Suppressor for above
Telescopic sight to suit above
Spare ammo
C3 putty explosives
Caps and detonators
Extra wire red, blue and yellow
1000 sheets with a message:-
"For every negro or black person that
is violated or tortured,
two Klansmen will be executed!
You have been warned!"

All the above to be secured in a false bottom in the trunk of a hired car that I can pick up at Memphis International long term parking.

Please inform me of the cover Hire Company you intend to use.

I'll make contact as soon as I'm installed and secure in Memphis.

Chapter 35

He posted a note to Jill that said he would be away on government business for a few days and asked her nicely to keep a fist full of notes from the course and drop off the letter he enclosed for the administration at the hospital.

On the Monday, Sam received confirmation that all his requirements were in place and that the cover hire people were Hertz. He took the flight to Memphis and arrived late afternoon, he picked up the modified car, checked the contents in the dummy tool box and found everything in place.

He drove to his pre–booked quaint little hotel about a half a mile from the professor's study.

He met Henry Langsdale at the vast entrance of Memphis University on Alumini Avenue, he was just what Sam expected, bespectacled, check shirt, tatty dicky bow tie and baggy brown trousers, a typical academic. Within a half an hour Sam was completely at home with the professor, nice guy thought Sam.

'Why don't you take a drive around tomorrow and see some of the wonderful places in our fair city and we can get down to work once you have relaxed a little' said Henry.

Sam drove out into the boonies taking in the shear natural beauty of the place when in the distance the sky took on a bright yellow/red glow. He stopped for gas and asked the old boy pumping the gas what the glow was.

'It's probably the Klan again burning crosses and lynching a couple of niggers' he said.

'They still do that? I thought those days were long gone, sounds bloody dangerous to me, I think I'll drive home' said Sam.

'Good night then young man and you take care Yah' hear.'

Sam turned the car towards Memphis and said goodbye. After about a half a mile he stopped did a U turn and headed for the haze in the distance. He parked the car in the trees in as much cover as possible, removed the rifle, silencer and telescopic sight and moved to a good shooting position. He looked through the scope and saw these strange looking creatures bowing and waving to the almighty.

The three leaders standing on a dais seemed to be directing things so became Sam's targets.

The Rifle was modified to take a clip of ten rounds, he zeroed in on the big fellow in the centre and squeezed off a round which hit dead center causing the white hood to turn a deep red, before the guy his the floor of the platform another prominent player followed him down blood pouring from a head wound. Panic started and men were running around in circles, Sam broke cover placed the rifle back in it's holder and closed the fake tool kit cover.

He grabbed a handful of hand outs and scattered them all around, then he was gone in a cloud of dust and heading for the freeway.

He kept to the speed limit all the way back to Memphis and his hotel, satisfied with his nights' work. That should put the cat among the pigeons, he thought.

He thought he would cover his ass just in case any police or FBI came sniffing around. He went to the front office in the hotel and saw the young clerk trying to keep his eyes open,

'I'm going across to the diner can I get you anything?' said Sam.

'A cheese burger would be nice thank you sir' said the guy whose name tag said Darren; 'Here's a tenner' said the young man.

'My treat' said Sam making his way through the swing doors, 'it's the first time I've been outside for ages', said Sam.

As Sam sat in a window seat watching the passing traffic a bunch of vehicles were speeding passed at 80 plus miles an hour, ambulances, police cars with sirens blasting out and what looked like standard FBI black vehicles joining the cavalry.

'What the hell is that all about?' one of the truckers said.

'Heard tell the Klan have some kind of a meet upstate tonight probably got there fire arms stuck in those dumb suits hey wear and shot themselves'. Said another trucker, "Fuckin' idiots". 'Either that or they set fire to themselves', he said laughing.

'Be careful what you say Richie, those bastards have got eyes and ears everywhere', said Bert the diner owner.

After Sam had finished his burger and fries he looked around the place and he was on his own, all the drivers away into the night.

'You got a strange accent young fella where you from?' said Bert.

'A little place in England called Poole, it's in Dorset county on the South coast, lovely place' said Sam.

'I think you've got a cheek Bert saying I've got a funny accent don't you think?'

'Maybe you are right he laughed' and sat down opposite Sam.

I'm here helping some old boy professor put together a book on the American Allies input into the fighting in the Pacific during WW2 especially Burma, where I was serving with the Royal Marines for four bloody years fighting the Japanese.' 'Fighting those little buggers was tough, their allegiance to their Emperor and country was total.'

Bert left to cook Sam's take away order for Darren. He popped the burger and fries into a doggy bag and gave it to Sam, 'This ones a "Freebie" enjoyed your company Sam' said Bert.

'I'll be here for a couple of weeks so I'll be a regular, good night Bert'. Sam left the diner and returned to the hotel dropped off the meal with Darren and went to bed.

He decided on the Tennessee Aquarium, the Babula Mexican restaurant in Overton Square, the Memphis Coffee Museum and a look at the three bridges that cross the Mississippi.

Sam worked with Henry for three days on the trot filling in spaces he had left open for the Brits, the Aussies and the New Zealanders participation in Burma.

'Have a day off Sam and we will see you at the country club on Saturday. It's a monthly dinner dance and all the local hierarchy will be there in all their glory.' said Henry.

Sam arrived early at the country club and sat adjacent to the foyer so that he had a good view of the arriving cars, the driver's and the passengers.

His wait was not wasted arriving in a fantastic white 8 cylinder Packard was the man himself, a self appointed bigot and 'Chief Wizard' Clyde Sinclair and his two thug sons.

Sam made a note of the number and followed the valet parking guy to where the vehicle was parked. The vehicle was parked quite close to Sam's car which made the transfer of the lethal explosive simple.

He placed the device under the floor between the front and the back seats using a simple magnet, the only thing left to do was flick the switch as the device was already time primed. He would return later to activate the switch.

The General had indicated that he had a trainee agent on the inside at the country club who although just a young man, was feeding good information on the K.K.K. back to him. The country club was a fine cover for upstanding Klan members. Sam established contact and they met in the parking garage.

'See this switch David?' said Sam pointing to the device, 'just turn it on prior to the Sinclair's calling for it', 'The delay time is twenty minutes so you are in no danger, are you OK with that?'

'Not a problem Sam' he said.

'Good man!' Sam finished and wandered back to the club to find Mr. and Mrs. Langsdale.

During the course of a very pleasant evening he crossed paths with the rookie agent who was now waiting on tables. Sam nodded his head towards the male toilets, the place was empty.

'I need a key to lock the toilets and a notice saying "This toilet is out of order please use the one in the Foyer, Many Thanks Management."'

'Not a problem Sam' said the rookie.

'Also lose the master key, until Monday at least' said Sam.

'Got it' he said and disappeared into the kitchen,

Also in the house were two Klan representatives from nearby Knoxville there to have talks with the Sinclairs. Knoxville recruitment was going well especially with young female Kluxers and junior Klansmen.

The place was emptying fast and the two heavy hitters from Knoxville entered the toilet, Sam followed them in locking the door behind him, he double tapped both men to the forehead with 9mm rounds from his Beretta, they both hit the floor and died instantly. Sam moved quickly to the door unlocked it and stepped out, then re-locked it.

David, right on cue, hung the "Out of Order" sign on the door handle. He gave Sam a nod and was gone in the direction of the garage. A call from the car valet service told David to bring the Sinclair's car. He reached under and flicked the switch to on and steadily drove the car to the waiting Sinclair's.

They roared off into the night waving at all the white people they could see and completely ignoring the black guys shoveling up the scattered tree leaves.

Sam said good night and goodbye's to the Langsdale's and said that he enjoyed working with the professor, Henry thanked Sam for his assistance in preparing the book and said that he would always be welcome back to Tennessee. Sam wasn't so sure about the last comment.

It was a quiet Sunday in Memphis for Sam, it was clear that the Saturday night take downs were to late to be reported for any Sunday editions.

Monday morning all hell broke loose, the Country Club was flooded with Local Police, County Police and the FBI, who had decided to take control. A TV reporter was interviewing a FBI Agent and she peppered questions at him.

'Lets calm down a bit, one question at a time please', he said,

'We have two bodies in the toilet area believed to be members of the Klan, they have both been shot in the head and the approximate time of death between 12 midnight and 2am Sunday.' 'The same "Two whites for one black" notes were scattered all over the toilet at random.'

'At this time it points to a vigilante group', he said. 'I will give you more information when I have it' he said walking away from the camera.

The TV girl presenter then caught up with the County Sheriff who was gently trying to make himself presentable before going in front of the cameras.

'At 4am, a bombed out Packard was found on route 70 approximately 15 miles out of town, we are trying to piece the body parts together as we speak, but the vehicle looks like it belonged to the Sinclair's, again the notes were scattered all around the crippled vehicle', he said.

That should reduce the numbers in the Klan s recruitment drive, thought Sam.

Sam started packing his bags for the trip back to California when the phone rang.

'Hello Sam Collins',

'Sam it's David at the country club'

'Where are you phoning from David', said Sam,

'Pay phone, down town Memphis',

'Good man, what have you got?' said Sam.

'I think we have stirred up a hornets nest they are hopping mad.' 'One of my informers has told me that the Tennessee Klan big wigs are holding a meeting in the church hall of the old Salem Baptist Church, South Memphis, it's just off route 70 south' he said. 'They plan to kick off at midnight.'

'Excellent news!' 'I'll take care of it, I want you to lie low and below the radar for a few days, I will inform the General of your first class work David, good man', Sam replaced the phone.

Wanting to get back to his studies he finished packing and reserved a seat on the midnight flight to LA. He released the catch on the secret tool kit box and transferred the remaining bomb making materials to his room.

When he had finished all that had to be done at the target was hook on the loose red wire to the caps and the yellow wire to the timing device.

It was 9pm when he arrived at the famous old church and he set to work installing the explosives. One in the empty water barrel, one in the boiler room and the final one hidden and lodged between some old unusable old furniture. Having satisfied himself that the devices were not easy to discover, he made the final connections adjusted the timing to 12.30 am and activated the devices.

Chapter 36

Sam left the car in the long Term Parking Area at Memphis International and then made the call to the General.

'Mission completed successfully Sir, the Klan recruitment plans I would suggest are on hold', said Sam. He continued 'The car is situated as per with the key on a magnet under the front fender', said Sam.

'Wonderful Job, I will not bother you for a year and by the way, good luck with your studies and your $25000 retainer is back in business, keep me in the loop Sam.'

Sam arrived back in LA early in the morning and took a cab to the marina boarded his lovely new home and went directly to sleep. The following morning Sam tuned in to the News Channel who were concentrating on the lethal bombing in Memphis. Seventeen Klan members had been killed and three more critical, the devices used were self made and not very sophisticated, probably made by some 'Black Power' or 'Black Freedom Fighter' group.'

'Our enquiries are well spread at the moment and the FBI have resumed control' said an Agent In Charge. He had two messages on his answer phone one from Jonny Li and one from Monique. Sam watched from the flying bridge as the delivery guy dropped off the daily newspapers outside the store. He ambled across picked up a Washington Post and a Memphis Daily News, he ordered a coffee and a bagel and settled down to read the detailed reports. He read the Headline '*The Ku Klux Klan in Memphis, Nashville and Knoxville have been devastated*". 'During the past week they have had 24 deaths and 4 still on the critical list. The FBI are stumbling around trying to avoid all out war between the Klan and Black separatist Groups.' 'We are concentrating our efforts on these Groups, but as yet no charges have been made' the Agent said.

Sam was pleased to have some time out to pursue his studies, he couldn't afford any more time away from the chalk face, he decided to give it a 100% effort to try and catch up with the rest of the trainees.

Chapter 37

Sam relaxed on the flying bridge and decided to concentrate on nothing but his anesthesia work, he returned to the hospital training centre on the following Monday and was pleased to see that the desk nearest to Jill's was still unoccupied.

'Nice of you to join us Mr. Collins' said the lecturer

'Nice to be back sir, I will for my sins be here for the next 12 months, if you can put up with me?' said Sam smiling. Sam was pleased to be back studying again, he was beginning to enjoy the company of the other trainees, especially Jill McGuire's.

Sam turned to Jill and inquired, 'Do you still require the "Collins Taxi Service" madam?'

'That would be great, thanks Sam'.

The weeks passed very quickly, two days at the chalk face, two days on the wards or in the theatre and Sam's beloved Thursdays which were Lecture free and more important a study day.

Sam was not surprised by his marks on his first few assignments they were down to 'C'-. This was OK, as he was still in catch up mode. physiology, chemistry and anatomy needed a lot more attention. The 'C'- could have been a lot worse if he hadn't received an 'A' for his practical skills handling the anesthesia enlistment.

During the next two months Sam developed a close relationship with Jill and they were becoming good friends. Her help on the three subjects where Sam was struggling was so important to Sam and he lived on every word that came out of her mouth. He was getting more confident as exam time approached.

One evening as he was dropping her off at her condo, Sam said

'How do you feel about coming over to the boat this weekend for a bit of joint studying?'

'I'd like that Sam, lets get your grades up' she said.

'OK, Friday straight from work and by the way I'm not hitting on you, it's not a date', he smiled.

'Bring along your books and notes, shorts, T shirts, bikini and your best frock we will need to go out to eat at sometime', said Sam.

'So we don't have to share a little single cot on your boat then?' she said with a cheeky smile.

'My boat is a 175 footer with 8 bedrooms all with "en suite" facilities. So I promise I won't lay a finger on you', said Sam still smiling. Jill laughed and returned to her studies.

Five thirty on the Friday they both strolled slowly to the car park and the MG both of them completely zonked. Sam placed Jill's case in the boot of the MG and they set off for the short journey to the marina. Sam parked the MG along side the boat and said 'There she is Jill, isn't she a beaut? Jill looked up at the magnificent craft her white highly polished hull glistening in the Marina's floodlights.

'She is beautiful, she's the most beautiful thing I've ever seen'.

'Come on lets get you aboard and settled'. After Jill had sorted herself out she returned to the lounge and sat down next to Sam cradling a Martini. They worked solidly for two hours, questions and answers and Sam taking copious notes.

'Love your company Sam but I've got to get to bed', said Jill.

'Go for it and thanks for helping me, breakfast at 9am, with plenty of coffee'.

In the morning Sam had prepared eggs, toast, orange juice and coffee as a puffy eyed Jill entered the galley. Apart from being a bit bleary eyed Jill looked terrific in a pair of little light blue shorts and a T shirt about three sizes to small to accommodate her ample bra less breasts.

'OK lets eat and drink as we go and get in some serious study time Sam.'

'A trade Sam.' 'I'll give you as much help as possible on the three, anatomy, physiology and chemistry if you go in depth with me on the anesthesia equipment, my grades were down in this' she said.

'You've got yourself a deal, we start at finishing time on Monday', said Sam.

They both worked solidly together for the next two months and Sam thought that if he wasn't ready for the year end exam he never would be, Jill was pleased with her progress with the equipment and was confident of a good grade.

The weekend prior to the year end exam paper, Sam caught up with his correspondence and wrote letters to Janet, Katherine, Lance, Trisha and Len confirming that he would be coming over to the UK for six weeks, starting mid July. The dreaded Tuesday arrived and all the trainees sat pensively and quietly in the lecture room hoping that the paper didn't vary to much from what they had concentrated on.

'OK people, you have four hours, you may begin', said the lecturer.

Sam took a deep breath and turned the question paper over. He scanned the whole paper and let out a whispered "Yes". It all fell into place and after three and a half hours Sam completed. He then carefully ran through all his presentation correcting some grammar mistakes and rearranging the layout to make it more professional. The bell sounded and everybody stopped working and handed in their exam papers.

All the trainees adjourned to the staff canteen where Jill made a beeline for Sam.

'Well how did it go Sam?' she said.

'Good, I may have got a 'B' said a radiant Sam.

'How about you then brains?' said Sam,

'You know me Sam got to be straight 'A's' she said.

After lunch, Sam got the call to complete the Practical Anesthesia Competency Test. Sam was confident he didn't leave anything to chance, he covered general anesthetics, spontaneous ventilation used mainly on emergency surgery, went through the basic principals (ANA), maintenance during the operation and completed by the emergence procedure. Turned off the equipment and removed the LMA when the patient wakes up. He left the theatre and said to himself 'that's an 'A'.

After dropping off Jill at her condo he returned to the boat and produced a poster. Front and centre was a picture of the "John Jo", the pier number and the birth number. He went across to the News Agents and took 30 copies. It read:

To say thank you to you all for putting up with me
this past year and helping me catch up.
I would like to invite you all to join me on my boat on
Saturday next for a snacks and wine party at 11am.
Please tick the box at the bottom of the page
if you can make it.

Sam Collins.

Sam arrived early on the Wednesday at the hospital and placed a poster on each individual's desk. He sat down still a little on edge with regard to his first year exam results. An envelope landed on everybody's desk with the exam results inside.

The confident trainees opened them immediately the doubters took there time. Sam slowly opened the envelope and there it was, Sam Collins would carry over to year two, a continuous assessment of 'B' plus.

The whole training centre was very quiet as everybody reviewed his or her marks. Suddenly Sam stood up and shouted out loud 'Yes!' The whole of the class turned and faced Sam and laughed out loud. The Chief Surgeon who was present during the hand outs, said,

'You seem to be happy Mr. Collins.'

'Surprised myself sir', said Sam.

'Oh and by the way, don't I get an invite to your soiree?' said Drew Cohen the surgeon.

'You and your wife would be most welcome', said Sam.

'We will be there'.

The Saturday brunch was a great success only four people were unable to attend. Dr. John and Monique were there and as with everybody else enjoying Manuel's Spanish and Mexican delicacies. At 1pm Sam announced that lunch was being served at "Filippo's" just across the way and anybody wishing to partake was welcome.

'Eat as much as you like, Sam's paying' he added.

Some people had to leave to catch planes or trains, so the final total sitting down to lunch was sixteen. After the meal everybody drifted off which left only Jill, John and Monique, he gave Jill a special hug and wished her a happy holiday and a safe trip back to Wisconsin.

Sam went back on board finished his packing for his trip to the UK, he was collected by Monique who took him to LA for his flight to New York. He flew into La Guardia, took a cab to 5th Avenue and phoned Chris and Mary Jo to set up a meet. The next day he spent some hours with the two girls at NYPD before departing for Idlewild and then on to London.

Chapter 38

Sam settled into a comfortable window seat as the Pan Am turbo prop aircraft reached it's cruising altitude and reflected on the air travel he made six years ago in the hold of a Dakota DC7.

They touched down at London International Airport right on schedule and Sam passed through immigration and customs without any hold ups. He made a call from the nearest pay phone,

'Hello Lieutenant Templeton'

'I need a bed, any chance Katherine?' said Sam,

'I recognize those Dorset dulcet tones, a bed is not a problem Sam,' she said.

'It's 22 Arcasia Avenue, Eltham, I'll see you there at around 5.30.' she said.

Sam made his way to Eltham and sat on a park bench waiting for Katherine to arrive. They embraced on the green outside Katharine's little cottage and she said how wonderful it was to see him again, they both sat down to catch up with things this side of the Atlantic and in the States.

'Daddy has been very ill and mummy and a nurse are taking care of him.' 'Lance's wife is expecting a baby and Trisha and David have adopted a little lad and I'm still single and working my ass off at the Admiralty', she said.

'You know of course of your mum's visit to New York, she wrote me and said that she had a wonderful time. She stayed with me in the penthouse on 5th Avenue', said Sam.

'I'm in my second year now studying for my CRNA degree in anesthetics, which as you know is something I've always wanted to do', said Sam.

'It was time for you to get out Sam and away from all that killing' she said.

'You are so right it was time to get out' said Sam.

'So how's your love life Katherine?' 'Any beau's on the horizon?' Said Sam.

'There is a guy showing a bit of promise, but its early days' she said.

I'll take you to Sunningdale tomorrow, mummy and daddy are really looking forward to seeing you, if you could spend a few days with them that would be great' she said.

'I need to get to bed, I'm shattered ', said Sam. Katherine gave Sam a little peck on the cheek and led him to the spare bedroom.

The following morning they drove to Sunningdale and Sam was greeted by an ashen-faced Sir Keith and his beautiful wife Janet. Sam saw immediately that Sir Keith was pleased to see him, for a brief moment his eyes came alive, he was sat in a wheelchair with a blanket over his knees and a large loud nurse who was piloting the chair.

Janet who was standing behind the two of them stepped forward and embraced Sam. That brought back memories thought Sam.

'Lets get inside, Lance is coming over for lunch', said Janet.

They all sat down and made general conversation.

'So, how's the treatment going Sir Keith?' said Sam.

'Seems to be the best yet, feeling a bit more energetic, always a good sign when I take a wee dram of brandy', he said with a grin.

'Good to hear sir' said Sam.'

'What are your plans Sam?' said Janet.

'I'm going to watch a bit of cricket at Lords, I especially want to see the Middlesex Twins, Compton and Edrich', said Sam.'

'I shall be popping in to see the Commander of MI5 in Curzon Street and paying a visit to the Commando school in Bickleigh to see my friend Len Jackson.' 'It would be nice if I could get to see Trevor and Trisha and their little lad' said Sam.

Sam stayed at Sunningdale for a week helping out with Lance on the upkeep of the grounds surrounding the Manor. It was good to get out into the fresh air and do some physical work.

'You'll need a car Sam, take the Healey', said Janet.

Sam said his goodbyes to everyone at the Manor and hit the A31 south to Camberley. He parked the Austin Healey close to the guard house and was confronted by a young second Lieutenant.

'Can I help you sir?' the young man said.

'My name is Lt. Colonel Lassiter RM, I did my training here many years ago and wondered if you could make enquiries with the C.O. to allow me in to see some long lost friends?'

'Just a moment sir', the young officer said moving over to a telephone.

'I'm so sorry Sir I didn't realise who I was talking to. The C.O is on his way down to see you'.

The Colonel burst through the guard house door and said;

'Sam it's good to see you'

'David Collingwood as I live and breathe' said Sam.

'It's got to be eight years since we were thrown together here at Camberley, still wet behind the ears', said the Colonel.

'A favour Sam, would you have a word with the latest bunch of officer recruits, strictly informal and off the record?'

'Not a problem David, I'll have some lunch and we'll get together in the mess, say 1400', said Sam.

Sam strolled into the Officer's Mess looking very elegant in his Italian suit, white shirt and Corps tie and asked a young serving waitress if her supervisor was on duty today.

'I'll just see sir' she said.

Trisha appeared and went quickly towards Sam's table.

'Is there a problem sir?' she said to the man at the table whose head was bowed

'Not really, bad supervision and bad service, nothing to worry about', said Sam.

'You bugger', said Trisha putting her arms around Sam and giving him a long protracted hug.

'it's wonderful to see you Sam how long are you in the UK?',

'I'm week 2 of 4, on my way to the Commando school to see Len', said Sam.

They talked for an hour, the main topic being young Thomas her little one. Sam gave her a kiss goodbye and went to the bar to greet all the new intake.

After an hour Sam was on his way again speeding passed Andover and on to Exeter, where he took the B road to Bickleigh He signed in and asked to see Colour Sergeant Jackson.

'He's on his way to see you sir', said the Corporal of the Guard.

Standing in the doorway of the guard house was Colours who threw up a salute 'Good to see you sir' said Colours.

'I've set up a table in the mess for a bit of scran Colonel, a lot of the young guns are eager to meet you', said Len.

'I've made the old General aware of your visit and he said he would drop by, "Ee'up" there he is now right on time', said Colours.

They made there way to the mess and were seated at a large table, the main topic being the fighting in Burma and the VC's.

Sam felt at home in this military environment and enjoyed answering the questions that were raining in on him. After two hours of questions and answers Sam stood up and said, 'My four weeks holiday are more or less over gentlemen, it's been a pleasure talking to you' said Sam.

Hand shakes all round prior to Sam's departure for Sunningdale where he would drop off the Healey.

The following morning Janet insisted that she drove him to the Airport, which they did in total silence, words weren't necessary, they both new how they felt about each other. Janet parked the car at London International Airport and retrieved Sam's case from the boot, handing it to him she said,

'You know I'll always love you Sam'. Sam took her into his arms and gave her a long lingering kiss. She smiled got in her car and was gone, tyres screaming.

'Back at you my darling Janet', said Sam passing through to Departures.

On the flight to New York he composed a letter to the General at the Pentagon saying that he wished to retire from the killing game and have some quality time and pursue his studies. On arrival at Idlewild he posted the letter before taking the New York Airways helicopter ride across Manhattan to La Guardia Airport.

The flight to LA was uneventful and Sam slept most of the way, when he arrived in LA he took the Greyhound to the Santa Barbara marina. He spent the next two days getting used to the temperature and time change taking a series of power naps.

Sam phoned Jill and they decided to meet and put together all the notes and text books required for the up coming term, apart from physiology, chemistry and anatomy they would be introduced to physics and biochemistry.

'I'll pick you up on Monday morning' said Sam.

Late on the Saturday evening Sam's phone rang, it was General Richards.

'Appreciate your letter young man, sorry to lose you, but I can understand' he said. 'I'm leaving your retainer in place as a bonus' he said. 'I'll cancel payments next April, it's easier for the accountant's, end of financial year and all that', said the General.

'You're a kind man sir and I hope a friend', said Sam.

'Both, I hope. Good luck'.

On the following Monday, the second year slog began, the continuous assessment was going well for Sam retaining his B plus grade. The pressure on two students who quit, but Sam and Jill loved the challenge, their confidence levels high.

Half term came which gave Sam a bit of a rest from his studies and he was able to spend time at Monique's studio doing odd jobs.

Christmas came and went quickly and Sam made a decision.

'I'm going to try for CRNA classification in June' said Sam to Jill.

'OK in for a penny in for a dollar', said Jill.

It was 15th June, 1947, Sam and Jill sat nervously in the examination centre anticipating the questions in the face down folders in front of them.

'OK people, Five papers to complete, three today and two tomorrow. Two hours per paper', he said.

'Ladies and gentlemen, you can begin.'

Sam slowly turned over the folder and pulled the first paper of the CRNA exam.

Physiology, Sam answered the questions and was reasonably satisfied. Chemistry was a breeze and anatomy gave Sam no problems. Fifteen minutes before the scheduled finish time Sam reviewed his three papers correcting and adding a few salient points. The papers were collected and all the trainees left the building.

'How did it go Sam?' said Jill

'OK I think, probably B's' 'What about you?' said Sam.

On the way back to Jill's condo Sam said,

'Do you want a run through on the mechanics of the anesthesia machines?'

'I think I'm OK Sam, thanks', she said.

'Good girl, I'll see you in the morning.'

'Good morning everybody!' 'I hope you all slept well after yesterdays heavy day, today we have two papers, two hours on each, physics and biochemistry.' '

'This afternoon it's a hands on examination with the anesthesia equipment.'

'You may begin', he said.

Sam recalled some of the physics in his Ordinary National Certificate (ONC) Mechanical Engineering, after finishing the paper he thought he may have pulled it off. The one worry Sam had was the biochemistry, a subject until recently he was not aware of. He did the best he could and laid out some constructive answers, although he was still not sure if his answers carried enough depth.

The hands on anesthetics examination was a breeze for Sam and he sailed through it. 'That's an 'A', he thought.

Sam and Jill met in the staff canteen and Sam was first to speak,

'Well it's done, I think the Bio' may be a tad tight, but I may have kicked it' said Sam.

'I was a little timid on the practical, let's hope I did enough', said Jill.

The weekend seemed to go on forever, Jill and Sam didn't talk to much, they preferred to suffer in silence. On the Monday Sam along with Jill sped quickly to Santa Barbara General. They both sat down in the training centre and waited pensively for the results to be posted. The results were brought in and posted on the giant notice board, the main body of students rushed over to see the results. There were cries of "Yes!" and "Shit!" as the students reviewed their results.

Jill slowly made her way to the notice board and the turned towards the still seated Sam gave him a huge hug and said;

'We both made it!' she said. Sam felt a moment of pride as he wiped a stray tear from his eye, looked at Jill whose face was completely saturated with tears of joy.

An official looking letter arrived on the following day from the Personnel Department of Santa Barbara General, It read:

Dear Mr. Collins,

We would like to offer you a permanent position in our Anesthesia Department.

After reviewing your results and especially your practical, Mr. Cohen the Chief Surgeon has recommended that you should be invited to join us.

Please arrange an appointment to come along and see me.

Regards
Personnel Manager.

Sam phoned Jill to put her in the picture and then phoned the personnel department for an appointment. Sam attended an Induction meeting for all new starters, then started his new career at a salary of $25000 a year.

Chapter 39

For the next two years it was the nearest to normality that Sam had ever been, a regular job that he loved, regular hours, and weekends with Monique and John and sometimes Jill and he kept in touch with his friends in the UK by writing regularly.

One weekend on the boat with Jill, both of them working on a sun tan, Sam all oiled up in his shorts and Jill in a bikini bottom and the same T shirt three sizes to small, just about covering her huge breasts.

'You're going to look a bit odd, with brown face, legs and tummy', said Sam.

'OK so cream me up' said Jill removing her T shirt and revealing two beautifully shaped breasts.

Sam gently applied the sun cream to Jill's back and then to her front. Jill was getting "Horny" her nipples standing out ready to receive Sam's due care and attention.

'Make love to me Sam'

It had been a long time since Sam had made love and he wondered if the same old problem would surface again. It didn't and the love making was wonderful. Jill not one of those fast and furious lovers, more a slow tempo and sensual one.

When they finished there love making Jill said,

'Thank you Sam, that was magical, it's been a long time.'

'Me too' said Sam.

The easy going carefree lifestyle of California was perfect for Sam, he was surrounded by friends and had the best living quarters in town. Christmas in 1949 was a quiet affair lunch and supper at John's place. Then back to business as the Doctor and his sister laid out there targets for the next year.

Chapter 40

Then one morning on the 25th July, 1950 Sam turned on the early news on the TV, to be informed that the United States had joined forces with the United Nations to rage war on the North Koreans who had attacked and breached the 38th Parallel.

Sam wrote to the Hospital Administration Department resigning his post, giving the mandatory one month's notice. He travelled to the recruitment office in LA and volunteered his services as an Anesthetist in the U.S. Medical Corps. He returned to the boat and sought out his old Marine equipment. He removed what he thought he may need in an emergency, although if he went to a M.A.S.H. unit they are non-combative.

Commando Knife, spare magazines 9mm, camouflage cream, mosquito protection cream, water and malaria tablets and other first aid items, he placed them all in a trunk,

addressed on the front:

The U.S. Army Medical Corps,
Mobile Army Service Hospital
UIJONGBU,
South Korea.

Sam reported to the U.S. Navy Depot in San Diego and collected his regulation Army gear, boots, shirts, fatigues and sweats, as a qualified CRN a nurse he carried the rank of sergeant.

He flew from San Diego to Tokyo and then on to South Korea in an old Dakota DC 7, he was traveling with ten other nurses all Lieutenants three of which were African Americans.

It was July 1950 when Sam touched down at a place called Taejon which was within 20 miles of the front line. His orders had been changed and he would now be working with the M.A.S.H. unit here in Taejon.

As soon as he arrived he was directed to a tent by a Corporal named "Chico",

'There is only one other medical Sergeant on the base, but you should be OK Sarge' it's a big tent', said Chico hiding a smile.

Sam dropped his bag off in his new quarters noting a hint of perfume as he left and familiarised himself with his new surroundings. He was a little apprehensive about his tent companion knowing that a lot of male Nurses were homosexuals, as long as the guy kept his distance Sam could live with that.

He saw a surgeon stop Chico and said

'I need a "Gas Passer" now! 15 minutes in the O.R. Sally is ill and I need a replacement!'

'Sergeant Collins are you up for this?' said Chico

'No problem, where's the O.R.?' said Sam.

Sam entered the tent adjacent to the operating theatre and scrubbed up and put on some sweats and a green face mask. Sam entered the O.R. and had a brief scan of the patient's notes, the patient, just a teenager, was lying on his back his chest a mass of blood. The surgeon entered the O.R with two pretty nurses, one on each arm.

'OK ladies lets get this kids chest open' said the surgeon.

'Put him to sleep Sergeant!' he said.

Sam moved into gear, mouth and nose mask on, gas in smoothly and efficiently he carefully maintained close vigilance during the four hour operation making small adjustments when needed to the patients needs.

During the operation the surgeon spoke;

'I'm David McLintock, people around here call me "Bird" because of my big beak I think, what do they call you young fella?'

'The name's Sam, Sam Collins sir'.

'The operation's complete' "Bird" said 'Lets close him up and then let young Sam bring him around.' There was blood all over the sheets, gurney, and the front of Captain McKlintock's white operating gown. Some even catching Sam in the face.

Sam brought the patient around talking to him throughout his recovery.

'Lets see those big brown eyes young man, come on back' said Sam.

'Welcome to Korea Sam' said the surgeon 'Good job!'

Sam threw his contaminated clothing into the basket and took a shower, if any of the nurses were watching, tough! Sam was so tired he really didn't give a damn. He returned to his tent and flopped on his cot and was out for the count, he woke up three hours later to find a lovely looking girl sitting on the end of her bed.

'We have a problem haven't we' said Sam.

'That depends on whether you snore or not?' she said.

'I'll move out in the morning, I can see why that Chico chap had a cheeky smile on his face when he directed me here' said Sam.

'I'm Desi Carpenter, anesthetist' she said,

'Sam Collins, the same'.

She moved her cot further away from Sam's and dropped the separation tarp to divide the tent into two equal halves.

'Lets give it a go Sam and if it doesn't work we'll try something else', she said.

'Want something to eat? I'm starving!' said Sam.

'Lets go, Sergeant Collins' she said.

The M.A.S.H. unit at Taejon consisted of one Colonel, two Majors one of which was Chief Nurse and the other an incompetent surgeon called Sidney Carrington.

Three other surgeons all Captains and ten nurses four of which were CRNA certified Anesthetists. There were a half dozen other soldiers attached to the unit and of course, the admin' guy, Chico.

The three Captains were the brains of the outfit with David "Bird" McLintock the nominated Head Surgeon, Captain Phil Naylor from San Francisco and Captain Brad "Mouse" Klinsman from New Jersey made up the quartet of surgeons.

The next morning Sam entered the O.R and started cleaning and maintaining the anesthesia equipment, a half an hour later Sergeant Carpenter appeared and joined Sam in his maintenance duties, just as they finished the main man "Bird" came into the O.R.

'Hello you two' he said,

Hi sir' they replied.

'The standard of surgery and equipment is not up to the standards you guys experienced back home, our job is to firstly, save lives and secondly, prepare the patients as best we can and get them either home or to Tokyo where that can receive more professional attention.'

'We do as best we can, but don't expect too much fancy surgery.' he said.

'We would like if it's possible sir, to review the patients notes prior to the op and spend more quality time with the patient during emergence?' said Sam.

'Excellent, no problems with me, Phil or Mouse' said the surgeon.

It was 5am on a cold winters day, when Chico got on the camp radio.

'All hands on deck, incoming wounded, a lot of them!' he said.

Bus loads of wounded were arriving, triage was established with Major Carrington in charge.

'What's happening in triage "Bird"? said Phil. 'I've got guys with minimal injuries on my gurney'.

'Me too' said Mouse. Captain McKlintock stormed out of O.R. and onto the bus which was the temporary triage area.

'What the fuck are you doing Major? There are guys out here with their guts hanging out and half their chests missing and we are fucking around with minor injuries!' said "Bird".

'There not Americans' said the Major.

'You get the hell out of here you are a waist of space, Ginger take command of triage' he said to the young African American nurse.

'I'm putting you on report Captain, gross subordination!' said the Major.

'You do that, you idiot!' said Bird and returned to the O.R., helping a nurse trolley through a gurney.

They finished the last operation at 4am, the four Surgeons completely exhausted, the nurses walking around in a daze and the four anesthetists making sure that all emergence's were successful.

That sorted, all apart from Sam went back to their tents.b Sam did a tour of the recovery patients ensuring that all was OK.

When they returned to there tent the centre dividing tarp was up and neatly secured, they didn't let it down, they simply went to bed and collapsed into a deep sleep, after a few hours sleep Sam awakened to find that Desi had moved her cot closer to Sam's and had her arm around his body.

I can live with that, he thought and went back to sleep. The following morning Desi and Sam never mentioned the cot moving but they both knew it was the beginning of a fine lasting friendship.

Sam was ordered to attend the Colonel's Office later that morning, Captains McKlintock and Naylor were stretched out in chairs along with nurse Ginger Baker.

Major Carrington was there, preening himself like a peacock with his only friend in the unit Major Lucy Sheppard.

'Sergeant Collins, Major Carrington has brought charges of insubordination against Captain McLintock, for his rant in the triage yesterday' said the Colonel, 'What's your take on this Sergeant?'

'If the triage had been conducted efficiently and correctly prioritizing the extents of the injuries, we could have saved the lives of three allied servicemen.' 'I reviewed the pre-op on the patients and concluded that if they had been moved to the front of the queue, they would have survived instead of being sent home to Australia in body bags sir.'

'You think so Sergeant?' Said an irate Major.

'I know so sir!' 'The only difference I would have made from what doctor McKlintock did would be to knock you out, not just asking you to leave '*Sir*'!' said Sam

'OK I've come to a decision.' said the Colonel.

'If you are prepared to drop the charges against Captain Mclintock, I will refrain from reporting you to the Army Medical Council for negligence on your part Major.'

The Major's face turned ashen as he left the Colonel's office with Major Sheppard's comforting hand on his shoulder.

'There will be other times Major' she said

There were no other times, as in mid 1952, Major Carrington was transferred back to the States and placed in an office job at Fort Worth. The most amazing thing was the transformation of Major Sheppard after the departure of Carrington, she became almost likable.

The Colonel, Captain Naylor and Captain "Mouse" Klinsman were also sent home after completing their tour of duty and were replaced by two young Surgeon Captains, Squires and Peacock.

The drop in the casualty rate gave Sam the time to catch up on his correspondence, he picked up a letter from

Monique who wanted to know when he was coming home and informed him that she had been depositing his yearly directors dividends for the last 3 years into his bank account in Santa Barbara.

At the last count, it was 2.2 million dollars!.

She went on to say that her brother had opened another clinic in Tokyo and was spending a great deal of time there. She left a phone number of the Tokyo clinic.

The second letter on the pile of unanswered letters was from Janet.

Dear Sam,

It is with sad heart I have to tell you that on the 10th May Keith passed quietly and peacefully away, he had been trying to beat cancer of the kidneys for 3 years. I'm sorry to burden you with such bad news.

When that dreadful war is over please come and see me!

Love Janet.

Sam replied to both letters and wrote a quickly to Colour Sergeant Len Jackson.

The war was dragging on relentlessly, the talks between the North and the South leaders going nowhere. The casualties thank god were getting far less and the M.A.S.H. unit settled into some kind of routine when "Chico" rushed into the dining tent and said,

'Major Sheppard and Lieutenant Kate Burns have not returned from R and R and are long over due, the fear is they have been abducted by the North Koreans somewhere between here and Pusan.' 'A message from an Infantry unit suggests they are being held captive at a village 5 miles from Pusan.'

The infantry Captain said he was so sorry but he would not be moving into that area for another week. Sam returned to his tent and studied a map trying to estimate where the two nurses were being held, he spotted a village 5 miles north of Pusan where according to the intelligence people the North Koreans had a small garrison.

For the first time in 3 years, Sam opened up his trunk and assembled what he thought he might need on his cot.

A double edged Commando knife, a 9mm silenced Beretta, six fragmentation high explosive grenades, camouflage cream, spare magazines of 9mm ammo and by 22:00 hours he was ready to travel the twenty miles in the hope of finding the girls.

He put on his well worn flak jacket, creamed up and left his tent leaving messages for Desi and Chico, he crept into Chico's tent and stole his two way radio then climbed aboard the jeep and set his course N-NE and left the compound.

He drove in the moonlight 18 miles N-NE, parked the jeep in the brush and covered it with a camouflage net, collected his kit bag from the rear of the jeep and started to jog the 2 miles to his target.

The North Korean garrison was quiet, he paused and surveyed. It was 1am when he silenced the first sentry, cupping his mouth he drew the knife across his throat.

His partner the second guard was strolling along smoking an awful smelling weed, Sam fired two 9mm rounds in his face and moved on to the temporary

Radio Room, sat in front of the radio his back to Sam was a young man, Sam put another two rounds into his back.

He passed a U.S. captured jeep and wondered if it was the one that the girls had used as he stopped outside the next tent and listened, some grunts of satisfaction from the two North Koreans who were shagging their asses off on top of the two American nurses.

Sam moved forward, the silenced Beretta at the ready, his foot caught a twig and it snapped alerting both of the soldiers, Sam shot the nearest one, the second man slashed his knife at Sam catching him a painful blow to his side causing a lot of blood soaking into his t- shirt and running down his body. He put two bullets between the guy's eyes. He went over to Kate who was shaking at the sight of Sam.

'It's OK Kate, it's me', Sam said. Delving into his kit bag for some first aid kits.

'Kate, patch up the Major as best you can, I'll be back in 10 minutes', he said.

Sam took four high explosive high fragmentation grenades with a seven second delay on them and threw them into the sleeping quarters of the north Korean Garrison, he turned away quickly and returned to the two girls.

Four huge explosions rocked the night, the only thing left of the Garrison was two large black charred holes. The three of them moved slowly towards the jeep, Sam helped Kate place the Major on the rear seat, his side was bleeding profusely, he would attend to it when they were out of danger. He drove the two miles to where he had hidden the other jeep and pulled the radio from the rear seat.

'Sam Collins to base, over'.

He repeated himself 'Sam Collins to base, over'

'Base to Sam, over' said Chico,

'We have a go situation here, I have the two girls and I will be with you in a half an hour, over' said Sam.

'Roger to that Sam, Captain McKlintock is standing by and Sergeant Desi is being patched through to Tokyo as we speak, over and out.' The radio went dead.

As Sam drove on towards the M.A.S.H. depot he got on the radio again.

'Sam Collins to base, over'

'Go ahead Sam it's Bird.'

'Sir, the two girls have severe facial damage, cuts and bruises, damaged genital and anal damage and probably the Major has a broken jaw, both have severe breast damage, a lot of bite marks over there entire bodies, over.'

'Got it Sam, see you in 20, over and out.

When Sam hit the M.A.S.H. compound the place was buzzing and in a flash the two girls were in intensive care having been injected with painkillers and stabilising drugs.

Sam was helped from the jeep by Desi who half carried him back to their tent, she took off all his blood stained clothes, cleaned up the stab wound, applied a local injection and stitched him up, she dressed the wound, slipped a clean pair of his underpants on him and tucked him up in bed.

'Thanks Des'. Said Sam slowly closing his eyes and going to sleep.

Desi said quietly 'I got your message through to Doctor Li.' 'Lt. Colonel Lassiter he will be arriving late afternoon today.'

At 5.30pm that day Doctor John's large Chinook helicopter touched down at the Taejon M.A.S.H. Base, he made his way urgently to meet Captain McKlintock.

'Let's see the patients, Doctor', said Doctor John to "Bird", 'Then I want to see my friend the Colonel'. 'This is the Colonel, Doctor' said the Captain pointing to the M.A.S.H. commander. 'Sorry!' 'Sam Collins I mean' he said.

After a long examination of the patients John had a talk with the Captain and the Colonel.

'I can make them beautiful again, if you agree it will take 6 to 8 weeks to complete. I will use my clinic in Tokyo,' 'By the way, Captain you did a nice job on the patients, excellent work!' said Doctor John.

'Now, where is Colonel Collins?' said John

'He's here and it's Sergeant you silly bugger' said Sam

John moved over to Sam and they held a prolonged hug,

'It's good to see you again Colonel', said Doctor John,

'It's good to see you again John, and it's still Sergeant', said Sam.

After a brief discussion it was agreed that the two girls would leave with Doctor John and that surgery would be carried out in Tokyo, Doctor John Li said that he would work on the two girls himself and that he would not accept any payment, the huge helicopters engines roared into life and in a moment was disappearing over the horizon.

Sam was making his way carefully across the compound not wanting to pull any stitches, when "Chico" joined him. They both reached the office to find the Colonel and "Bird" sitting down each cradling a scotch.

'I have a wire sir, it reads "An Australian Infantry company patrolling in the Pusan area have come across 27 dead north Koreans and a burned out tented area. No one has taken responsibility of the attack, it remains a mystery. We did find blood soaked ladies underwear in the only tent left standing, so we are sorry to say that there is no trace of the two missing girls."

Six weeks later the Major and the Lieutenant arrived back at the Taejon MASH unit to thunderous applause from the 100% turn out of M.A.S.H. Personnel.

Both the girls looked radiant and beautiful, Doctor John had done a wonderful job on the restoration, the two officers went directly up to Sam and gave him a huge hug with tears streaming down their faces.

Sam satisfied that the raid on Putan would be kept secret, severed his duties with the U.S. Medical core, said his goodbyes and left for Tokyo to meet up with John Li.

Chapter 41

Sam left Korea and took a flight to Tokyo, he was met at the airport by his great friend Doctor John Li and they travelled to the heart of the city by cab and checked in at the Holiday Inn.

At dinner that evening John asked Sam to come and work for him as an anesthetist floating between his clinics in Santa Barbara and New York City.

'It's not so rough and ready that you have been used to for the past 2 or 3 years, but it will keep you off the streets and ease yourself back into civilization. What do you say Sam?' said John.

'I say yes and thank you John' said Sam.

'OK take a break and report for duty after Christmas, let's start you at 50,000 dollars a year, are you happy with that Sam?' said John.

'More than', said Sam.

After watching John perform in his clinic a few times during the next couple of days Sam left for the States, he took a flight to San Francisco and then the Greyhound to Santa Barbara Marina. He sat down in his beautiful lounge on his beautiful boat and relaxed for the first time for a long time.

Christmas was spent quietly at John's home up in the Santa Barbara hills with Monique and her new boyfriend, Manuel his wife and his children, presents were exchanged as everybody sat around digesting the superb meal prepared by Manuel. Sam spent most of the time with Manuel's two boys playing with a newly acquired train set.

The weekend prior to Sam starting work with Doctor John, he walked over to the U.S. Postal to buy some stamps and post some letters to the UK, he stopped briefly at the notice board and saw an ad:

"For Sale a Ferrari Monza, 21000 miles, price $80,000. Come on over to pier 20 and take a look at her."

Sam walked around to pier 20 and there it was the most beautiful beast in the world.

'Do you like her, she's a beauty isn't she?' said a guy sitting on a sun bed.

'She certainly is', said Sam.

'Hey, aren't you the guy that has just returned from Korea, the guy on the "John Jo"', he said.

'That's me, Sam Collins.'

'Have you still got the little MG?' 'I'd love to have that TF in my collection!' he said.

'Yes she's parked up and looking in mint condition' said Sam.

'I'll tell you what I'll do Sam, I'll trade you the Ferrari for the MG plus $50000 have we got a deal?'

'We've got a deal' said Sam shaking the guys hand.

It was early in 1953 when Sam started working with Doctor Li and the other surgeon's at his Santa Barbara clinic, a different approach was needed for the clientele he was now administering to, these ladies had loads of money or their husbands did and had to be treated with kid gloves on, nice words of encouragement prior to putting them under and even nicer words on emergence. The clients were treated like royalty, slightly over the top of course, but good for business.

On his off days he would either keep up the maintenance on the boat or help out with jobs that needed doing at Monique's studio.

One day he was decorating the rear parlour when Monique announced that she had become engaged to one of her brother's young plastic surgeons, Sam gave her a hug and said that he was happy for her.

Sam wrote to all his friends in the UK informing them that he was back in the States and enjoying the casual laid back California life style.

A letter arrived from Janet who said that she now had a life of a lady of leisure now that Lance had taken the responsibility of running the estate.

Sam read the last paragraph of her letter where she said that she still reserved a place in her heart for him. It was time thought Sam to tell the lady what he truly thought. He made himself comfortable and composed a letter to Janet.

My Darling Janet,

I'm not sure how Lance and Katherine are going to take what I have to say, it may be embarrassing for you, but my life without you for these past few years has been a killer for me.

I want you to come and live with me in California and I would like you to become my wife.

Ever since you glided through the arrivals at the Airport in New York seven years ago I've wanted to be with you.

I have enclosed a photo of what your new home looks like if you decide to take up my offer.

You can call me at anytime with your answer.

I will always love you. Sam.

Two days later Janet phoned and said that she would love to come to America and be his bride and it would be the happiest day of her life, she went on to say that both Lance and Katherine were as thrilled as she was.

She concluded by saying she would arrive in LA next Saturday evening.

'I love you to bits' she said and ended the call. Sam had never been so happy in his life and spent the next few days with a smile on his face.

'You look happy', said Doctor John,

'More than happy John, I'm getting married to the lovely Janet, so brush up on your best man duties!' said Sam.

On the following Saturday morning Janet said goodbye to Lance and Katherine and drove to the main gate and picked up the new gate man, he would return the Austin Healey to the manor after setting down Janet at the airport.

Janet was an excellent driver and was cruising at a steady 60 miles an hour on the way to London on the A31. She dropped a gear to take a blind bend only to be confronted with a thirty ton articulated lorry that had "jack Knifed" and heading straight towards her., the head on impact must have been at 100 mph and the Austin Healey was a crumpled mess with steam rising from the smashed radiator when the police and the ambulance service turned up.

Both Janet and the passenger were pronounced dead at the scene, both deaths were instantaneous, Janet's passport was found amongst the wreckage and Lance and Katherine received the terrible news.

Autopsies were carried out on the two bodies before being taken to the funeral directors in Sunningdale.

'We need to phone Sam!' said Katherine,

'You do it Kate, I can't handle that', said Lance. It was 3am when Sam's phone rang and thinking that it may be Janet calling picked up the phone in one swift movement.

'Good morning Sam speaking!' he said,

'Hi Sam it's Katherine, it's not a good morning Sam in fact it's a shitty one', she said.

'There's been an accident, mummy was involved in a head on smash with an arctic on the A31 just outside Staines, she was killed instantly.' 'It's a tragedy for the whole family and especially you Sam darling, I am so, so sorry!'

The silence went on for an age, it was finally broken by Sam who said,

'I have never loved anybody so much as I loved your mother, I must put the phone down and have some quiet time and remember all the wonderful moments that we had together', said Sam.

'I won't attend the funeral, I'd be in bits', he replaced the receiver.

Sam sent a two dozen red roses via the international florists with a message:

To my darling Janet, I will always love you. Sam.

For many days and nights Sam thought about Janet every day, remembering the good times they had together, in an effort to get some kind of closure.

In the ensuing months, John and Monique were very supportive and adopted him as part of the family. When the rotation took him to New York he met up with Chris and Mary Jo at NYPD the three of them went out to dinner where Sam told them about Janet's death.

'We became good friends you know Sam, we corresponded many times.' '"Jesus" I can hardly believe she's gone', said Chris, they both went over to Sam and wrapped there arms around him.

A few months later Sam was reading the maintenance manual for the Ferrari, when he glanced up at the TV News, the leggy blonde reporter was interviewing a FBI Agent.

Sam turned up the volume and sat down to listen to the report. The FBI guy said 'At 7pm last evening a drive by shooting took place at Gino's Bar on Ocean Boulevard.' 'A dark coloured muscle car with four black guys sprayed the front area of Gino's with over hundred rounds, shattering the front window and killing eight LAPD officer's, with five more in intensive care at LA General.'

'At this point in time, we think that they are revenge killings relating to the so called heavy handedness of

LAPD officers when they arrested a prominent gang member' 'if you remember the guy died in custody', he said'

'The car used in the attack was ditched and abandoned in South LA.' 'The FBI will be taking overall control of the situation', he said.

His thoughts were interrupted by the phone ringing.

'Hi this is Sam Collins',

'Hi Sam Collins, this is Monique Li',

'I want you to take me to LA, I want to go shopping big time and I want to spend a lot of money', she said.

'I'll call for you in 20 minutes' said Sam.

Sam pulled up outside the studio in his gleaming Ferrari Monza Spider

'Wow, when did you get that beauty?', said Monique.

'This is it's first day out, lets enjoy it' said Sam.

Monique was piling up all sorts of expensive designer gear in one of the top shops on Rodeo Drive.

'You go take a coffee Sam and when you return I'll put on a fashion show', she said. Sam was just crossing the street when he saw a rough looking guy looking at his Ferrari.

'What do you think of her?' said Sam.

'Nice motor!' came the gruff reply in a strong accent, probably Romanian or Russian.

'0 to 60 in 5 seconds' said Sam.

'Nice motor!' he repeated and strolled to a car parked next to Sam's and sat in the driving seat. Strange guy thought Sam, as he continued his walk to the up market cafe. Monique appeared in the window of the shop and beckoned Sam over, Sam sat down and waited for the show to begin.

Monique disappeared behind a curtain,

'Wow, you frightened me to death', she said to the young lady crying and cowering sitting cross legged on the floor.

'What's the matter honey?' said Monique

'I sorry, I don't speak the good English', she said,

'That's not a problem ma'am, lets get you a drink of water', said Monique leading the lady out from behind the privacy curtain.

The girl serving said she would see the woman out.

'You won't see her anywhere young lady she's with me', said Monique sitting the woman down at an adjacent table.

'Sam, your help is needed' said Monique.

'What's your problem Ma'am?' said Sam.

'If that ugly man there see me talking to you, I'm dead and so is my man' she said. Pointing to the guy who was inspecting the Ferrari.'

'My husband is clever man he's accountant for Russians.' 'But after last night's killings he want out, we both want out but it very difficult to leave the mob!' she said.

'What has last nights cop killing to do with it?' said Sam. 'And there is a way I can get you both out of there', he said 'Tell your husband to call me Friday evening, not from your home, from a pay phone, I 'm in a position to help you', said Sam.

Sam's phone rang at 11.30,

'Hello Sam Collins',

'Hello Mr. Collins, my name is Nikolai Trechicov' 'You spoke with my wife earlier today, she said you can help us?' he said.

'I can help you Nikolai but it's a two way street, I need some good stuff from you.' said Sam

'I work for the United States Secret Service and I can set up a witness protection scheme for you, we need to meet', said Sam.

'There is an all night diner at Beach and Dearborn, I can be there in one hour, people say I look like an accountant and I'll be wearing a green windcheater', said Nikolai.

They met and talked for an hour and Sam learned why Nickolai wanted out, they went too far when they gave $100,000 to the 'Gang Bangers' to carry out the drive by.

'I passed the money on to Vernon Johnson the leader of the gang called Level 42.' 'I have brought along my ledgers for you to take and I will bring all illegal money transfers to district judges, lawyers, paralegals and several police officers, after I have heard your proposals.'

'Your wife tells me that the annual visit for all the wives and kids to Disneyland is still on for this weekend, is that so?' said Sam.

'That is correct, and I am playing golf with some of my legal friends on Saturday.' said the Russian.

'Excellent, instead of playing golf get all your things together and report to the Santa Barbara Marina and go aboard a boat called the "John Jo" on Pier 19. at 4pm.'

'I will be on board to welcome you together with the FBI who will after a short meeting make you both vanish within the Witness Protection Program.' said Sam.

'Drive carefully and be safe!' said Sam.

Sam returned to his boat it was 1am when he made his first phone call to General Richards.

'Hello sir, it's been a long time, Sam Collins here'.

'What can I do for you Sam?' said the General.

'You can put me back on the payroll sir, I have a good take on the police murders here in LA'.

'Just put me on a retainer sir and change my ID back to Lassiter, I think people have forgotten my past track record.'

'I'll see to it Sam, welcome back!'

Sam then placed a call to Bert Lansing the FBI Agent in Charge of the LAPD massacre.

'Agent Lansing, my name is Sam Lassiter and I work for the US Secret Service, this can be verified by phoning General Richards at the Pentagon.' said Sam.

'What have you got for me Sam?'

'Enough to take down the Russian Mafia and a few so called loyal American citizens', said Sam.

'Can you get over to see me tonight, I'm on my boat the "John Jo", pier 19, berth 7, Santa Barbara Marina'.

'I'm on my way', said the FBI Agent.

Sam gave Bert a beer and they sat down to chat, Sam producing the ledger he acquired from Nikolai, the clearly stated ledger detailed payments made to people in high places.

'This is dynamite Sam!'

'Lets put in place a time table, which we must strictly adhere to'. Said Sam, 'Saturday morning at 4am Nikolai and his wife arrive here at the boat, he drops off all the money transactions over the last five years, we talk to him and you can satisfy yourself that he can be slotted in to the WPP', 'You will get in position to make all the arrests of the guys taking back handers, while I travel to Catalina and destroy their stronghold.' 'The only help I need from you Bert is for you to supply me with an

Agent who can swim, use a computer, and doesn't get sea sick', said Sam.

'Just a little bit of info for you Bert, the Russians gave the Level 42 gang $100,000 to carry out the drive by, it's all in the paperwork you now have in your possession.'

'I need six high explosive devices for the trip to Catalina, can you help Bert', said Sam.

'They will be here at 4am on Saturday along with Sandra Bishop an excellent agent'. said Bert.

Nikolai had free licence to transfer any mob monies around to achieve a higher percentage gain, so he emailed the bank, using a code to transfer all mafia accounts to a Washington holding account, he would arrange the various investments later in the morning.

Within seconds the money was transferred to a secret service account in Washington, they both wished the Russian good luck and the witness protection guys took over, the procedure was carried out with the utmost precision.

When Nikolai left Bert and Sam went through the paperwork he had left, leaving nothing to chance, the FBI man spotted the payment details to Vince Chavez the leader of Level 42, this was confirmation that the Russians had ordered the drive by.

'All the women and children are off the Island and I intend to pay them a visit, if I fail Bert you can move in with the cavalry.'

'OK what do you need Sam?' said Bert.

'I need an overall plan of the site, some scuba gear and as I said before, six high explosive devices, preferably C4 with timing options.'

On the Saturday morning an attractive young fit looking Agent turned up at the Marina,

'Hi Mr. Collins my name is Sandra Bishop FBI', she said.

'Hi Sandra Bishop FBI welcome aboard', said Sam. 'Take a memo Miss Bishop' said Sam.

The Russian Mafia paid the Gang Bangers of Level 42 $100,000 to carry out a drive by and murder eight LAPD officers.

The FBI has names and will be making arrests later today. At the same time as these arrests, I will be taking care of business on Catalina island, the mob's stronghold.

If you want to see the fireworks ensure you have a chopper in the air with a good camera guy just after midnight tonight.

'OK Sandra this note to be wired to KYTV News Room Los Angeles at 11.30 this evening', said Sam. 'Lets get the gear together and put it aboard the little boat Sandra.'

While Sandra was loading up the little fishing craft, Sam familiarised himself with the layout of the mafia estate on Catalina island, he made a mental note of where to place the high explosives to cause the most damage.

The explosive devices arrived on time and were transferred to the little boat and by 9pm Sandra and Sam were on their way for the 22-mile trip to Catalina. Sam had decided to make his point of landing the next bay along from the target area.

At 10.30 they dropped anchor in a group of six other boats hired out for a nights fishing, Sandra baited the four fishing rods and expertly cast them into the ocean. Sam put on his wet suit, flippers and collected his waterproof bag housing the explosives and then dropped over the side and swam underwater for the half mile to Catalina. He beached and stowed the bottles and flippers and made his way to the first bomb placement.

There seemed to be a bit of a drinking party going on in one of the buildings, probably vodka the Russians favourite tipple. All devices located, primed and the timing coordinated, he retraced his steps back towards his wet gear.

Two giant figures were standing smoking near Sam's stash, he approach the two big guys from the side and shot them both in the head at close range with his silenced Beretta, he dragged the bodies into the undergrowth, donned his wet gear and made his way underwater back to the John Jo 2.

At 11.15 he was back on board, Sandra pulled in the rods, started the engine and directed the craft towards Santa Barbara.

'Take over Sam, I'll get off the note to the TV station.' Fifteen minutes later they both looked up as two noisy helicopters passed overhead with KYTV clearly printed on each.

At 12 midnight what sounded like a thunder in the distance was picked up by Sam followed by the distant sky going a bright yellow and then settling to a red glow, Sam and Sandra punched fists and continued their journey back to Santa Barbara Marina.

They secured the little fishing boat to the stern of the "John Jo", stashed the gear and made there way on to the luxury cruiser. Sam turned on the TV and selected the KYTV News Channel, the reporter was getting really excited as he leaned out from the chopper.

'Tonight I have witnessed the total destruction of the Russian mafia's stronghold on Catalina island, as you can see not one building is standing, you can see many bodies lying near the buildings ruins.'

'This action was taken after proof of the Russian mafia's involvement in the killing of eight LAPD police officers.' said an FBI Special Agent in Charge.

Sam picked up his encrypted phone and dialed the TV station.

'News desk please' he said. 'I appreciate you keeping "Mum" on the information that I have supplied to you, but I need you to do me one more favour', said Sam.

'Please broadcast this statement:'

Any member of the Russian Mafia that is still standing has 48 hours to get out of southern California.

If you do not leave, you will be hunted down and executed. You have been warned.

Sam and Sandra were feeling a little tired and were having problems focusing on the TV. Sam fell asleep on the large comfortable sofa, Sandra covered him with a sheet and slid in next to him and went to sleep.

The following morning Sam went to the galley and put on the coffee leaving Sandra sound asleep on the sofa. 'Coffee Sandra' said Sam as he tuned in the TV to KYTV "Good Morning Los Angeles". The Reporter standing amongst the ruins of the once stronghold of the Russian Mob said,

'Last evening an attack was made by an unknown body of men on the Catalina stronghold of the Russian Mafia, all five properties have been completely destroyed, twenty seven bodies have been found in the wreckage.'

The camera panned the area identifying many body bags. The reporter then introduced Bert Lansing the FBI Agent in Charge of the LAPD murders.

'Military explosives were used by the attackers which points to some vigilante ex military guys carrying out this destruction', he said 'We will continue in our search to try to find the perpetrators.'

'We have made several arrests of prominent people in our area, one judge, three paralegals and seven renegade cops.'

'They have already been charged and sit in prison awaiting trial', said Bert, 'How we received the tip off and where it came from is our business and not for general publication', Bert concluded.

'Keep it here on KYTV if you want to hear the whole story of the Russian Mafia melt down', said the reporter 'This is Sally Ryder returning you to the studio.

'It was cool working with you Sandra you are a credit to your outfit, I'll pass that on to your peers', Sam said.

'Thanks Sam it was great working with a real pro!.' she said.

Sam and Sandra went over to "Filippo's" for breakfast when Sandra turned to Sam and said,

'I apologize Sam I'm not the real deal at the moment I'm having trouble with closure on the death of my fiancee, he was a good FBI agent Sam.' 'He was gunned down by some drugged up thug when the mission went tits up', she said.

'I can sympathize with you Sandra I too have a closure problem, my beautiful bride to be was killed in a RTA in the UK on her way to the airport.' 'She was coming to California to get married to me.'

'I think of her all the time, it just won't go away', said Sam. As they walked back to the boat Sandra turned to Sam and said.

'What do you think that we try to beat this thing together', she said 'I need to try something!'

'lets give it a go', said Sam.

The sun was just coming up over the horizon as Sam and Sandra stood on the flying bridge looking out on the ocean. Sam put his arm around Sandra's shoulder and she moved in closer to him and put her arm around his waist.

'Maybe, just maybe, maybe we can, yes, let's give it a go Sandra.'

LASSITER RM.
Robert C. King

Lightning Source UK Ltd.
Milton Keynes UK
UKOW01f2147260416

273022UK00001B/6/P